Lion Mountain

Lion
Mountain

Mustapha Tlili

Translated from the French by

Linda Coverdale

Arcade Publishing · New York

Little, Brown and Company

FIRST ENGLISH-LANGUAGE EDITION

The characters and events in this book are fictitious. Any similarity to real persons, living or dead, is coincidental and not intended by the author.

LIBRARY OF CONGRESS CATALOGING-IN-PUBLICATION DATA

Tlili, Mustapha, 1937–
   [La montagne du lion. English]
   Lion mountain / Mustapha Tlili; translated from the French by Linda Coverdale.
   p. cm.
   Translation of: La montagne du lion.
   ISBN 1-55970-056-4
   I. Title.
PQ3989.2.T58M6613   1990
843 — dc20   90-30278
                       CIP

Published in the United States by Arcade Publishing, Inc., New York, a Little, Brown company.

Originally published in France by Editions Gallimard under the title *La Montagne du Lion*.

10 9 8 7 6 5 4 3 2 1

Designed by Barbara Werden

FG

Published simultaneously in Canada by Little, Brown & Company (Canada) Limited

PRINTED IN THE UNITED STATES OF AMERICA

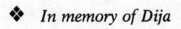 *In memory of Dija*

Author's Acknowledgments

I WOULD like to thank Sterling Lord for his belief in my work, and I wish to assure him of my faithful friendship. My thanks go also to Richard Seaver for his special care in editing this English-language version of my novel. My affectionate friendship is also for Jeannette Seaver, for whose encouragement I am forever grateful.

I
Ocher

THAT HORIZON, where our ancestors suddenly appeared one day, gave this village its name.

Lion Mountain.

Everything here is imbued with the legend of those founding fathers, those learned warrior-lords, the Ouled El-Gharib.

For the villagers, this past, which they both fear and respect, though it lies beyond their powers of comprehension, governs their lives. The little mosque is there to remind everyone of this heritage and dispel any doubts that might trouble an unwary mind. A dusty building, poignant in its simplicity, sparsely decorated and quite humble, with clumsy, uneven lines of the utmost severity. Beautiful, however; strangely, awkwardly beautiful. Unforgettable. Walls and minaret of ocher, like the Mountain. Cupolas of a washed-out white, faded by the rains and sandstorms. The blue doors and windows are crackled, bleached by the burning sun. Yet the mosque is the shining source of a matchless authority, a beacon for every heart and mind.

And the wanderings of the small stream? Isn't there a lesson to be learned from them? The brook flows past the house of Horia El-Gharib, gently at first, aimlessly, as though content simply to provide pleasure. After meandering along through the rocky waste, where it sparkles with a thousand glints of silver and gold, its course runs by the mosque, about two kilometers downhill, thus enabling the faithful to perform their ablutions and fulfill their duty toward God. The stream then wends its merry way across the fertile section of the village, irrigating orchards of pomegranates, figs, almonds, mulberries, peaches, plums, apricots, and other fruit trees. Beneath their boughs, in square plots artfully marked off by channels providing a thin but precious trickle of water, grow abundant tomatoes and pimientos, parsley, carrots, and turnips, and all kinds of melons. The stream provides the villagers with the fruits and vegetables of every season, the means to live in moderate but honest comfort, and a constant motive for pious gratitude toward the ancestors who sleep for all eternity beneath the sacred domes close by.

ACCORDING to one fanciful account of the past, the spring that feeds the stream gushed forth just as the first horseman galloped out of the unknown. Pondering the meaning of all she saw around her, there were times when Horia El-Gharib had no hesitation about placing her trust in this version of events. Whenever she contemplated the life-giving brook on which everything depended; whenever she considered how ardently the village dwellings huddled around the mosque, forming an impregnable semicircle embraced in turn by another crescent of verdant land, rich in the good things of this earth; whenever she reflected on the destiny of all those people whose arduous lives were inspired by faith, guided both day and night by the mingled rituals of irrigating their farmlands and heeding the muezzin's calls to prayer in preparation for the hereafter; whenever, in short, Horia thought about that web of connections, of secret complicities, of diffused but real interdependence that bound together orchards, houses, mosque, and villagers, she could only marvel at it all. Why not believe the ancestors had meant it to be this way from the very beginning? she would ask herself, musing over the warm, densely woven texture of so many mysterious relationships. From the moment they first appeared on the horizon, the ancestors had known what future to bequeath their descendants. Thanks to their sacred power, they had commanded the water to bring prosperity to this land. In Horia's eyes, this green, white, and ocher village dominated by a slender minaret, blooming miraculously in the vast and flinty wasteland, bore witness to the genius of the ancestors and the prudence of their vision. For her the village was simply an extension of these learned warrior-lords, the repository of their heritage, of their values: hierarchies of what was lawful and unlawful, good and evil, true and false. She often used to tell me that everyone in the village knew this, even when he strayed or sinned. She believed in a clear and deliberate order of things, an order that had reigned ever since the birth of this miracle in the wilderness.

IMAM SADEK, who has been the imam of Lion Mountain for more than forty years, is the ultimate judge in matters of great moment. Some people claim he is older than most of the village elders. For everyone, the imam is the voice of our ancestors, assuring their continuity as the latest in an unbroken line of religious leaders that stretches back for centuries. Knowledge and faith. Order and law. Peace and justice. If the mosque is the center of Lion Mountain, Imam Sadek is the center of the mosque. When he speaks, the people listen with devotion, respect, and fear. His sermons on Friday pour soothing words of wisdom over confusion and troubled passions.

And so no one was surprised when the imam delivered a homily in the presence of the very first "Delegate," the representative of the nation's new masters, in which he praised the French for having refrained, as he put it, from interfering in the village's affairs, at least in peacetime. Confronted by arbitrary rule and its misdeeds, the imam urged the populace to resist. The new authorities backed down, and no one ever learned the real reasons behind this retreat.

❖ 2 ❖

THE WINDS of change that swept over this part of the world hardly touched the village at first. After the initial crisis that sparked the village's defiant stand against the country's new leaders, Lion Mountain was left to itself once more, despite its location on an important road: the Great Highway, also known as Highway 15.

This new government isn't the only one to have left Lion Mountain in peace for a while, as I said. The French before them had completely ignored the village for almost the entire time they ruled the country. Were they moved by the unexpected sight of dwellings clustered jealously around the little mosque and nestled in a mass of green that stood out like a question mark against the endless lonely plain? Had they preferred to contemplate this scene of rare beauty from afar? I will simply note that they took up residence very near the source of the spring, at the other end of Highway 15, our one and only asphalt road, which the French themselves had built. Coming up from the south, the road runs at a slight elevation along the village's western flank before climbing northward to pass about a hundred meters in front of Horia's house, then continues past a few European buildings — the school, the post office, the former police station that served for a while as the new government's headquarters but which is now completely dilapidated — and the few surviving poplars from a magnificent row planted along the uphill side of the stream by the French soon after their arrival, as a source of shade and a reminder of the country they had left behind. The highway also runs by the little hotel, where wine is still served in this Muslim country, oddly enough, and where I sit writing these words; then the road sets out to conquer the rest of the wilderness and the country's arable land, following a winding course that plunges deep into the secrets of the blue mountains.

THE OLD French quarter is called "the Spring." It's the modern section of the village, even though it now lies partly in ruins. One could draw an almost perfect equilateral triangle between the Spring, Horia's house, and the small group of traditional dwellings. The old woman's house would be at the apex, while Highway 15 would form the base as it runs past, linking together the original village and the European neighborhood. Opposite Horia's house looms the Mountain. It makes an imposing and unusual boundary at the western edge of the property that begins at the house and extends a good two kilometers on the other side of the highway. Up until the dramatic events related in this narrative, the great stretch of land lying between Horia and the Mountain had remained intact, untouched by any cultivation or construction.

Seen from Horia El-Gharib's house, with its view unobstructed by the slightest natural or artificial obstacle, the Mountain was inexhaustibly beautiful.

A GEOGRAPHY more than physical or human: sacred. At least until the tragedy. Yes, that's the way it really was for the villagers. In their vision of the world — and above all in the eyes of the imam, that vigilant guardian of the Law — the natural order of things was profoundly at one with the moral and judicial orders. In this mystical topography, landmarks determining the rights of each and every individual were perfectly clear. And so on the eve of the events that would abruptly call into question a good many truths, everyone knew that the rise of land sweeping from Horia's house up to the Mountain was the legitimate realm of the old woman, as it had been for her family before her, and for their ancestors from time immemorial. No one needed to discuss or prove this, for it had always been so.

❖ 3 ❖

BUT THE PEOPLE of Lion Mountain were mistaken, badly mistaken, and when I ask Imam Sadek to explain what has happened, he will choke back his tears and say: "The world has gone mad, my son."

Yes, the ancestral certainties that recognized as self-evident Horia El-Gharib's right to her land and to her pristine view of the Mountain fell victim to the madness and folly of the world.

Those who, like Horia's elderly servant Saad, thought that everything that was legitimately yours would always be yours, were also proved wrong.

Everyone in Lion Mountain was wrong. Horia would say that they "erred." The old woman suffered the tragic consequences of this error in her flesh. Mistake, gunfire, blood. Blood for an ocher mountain.

❖

AFTER HORIA, after Saad, today it is my turn to die. The time has come to depart forever. To say farewell.

Farewell, beloved land! Village of happiness — farewell! I must resign myself, stifling every sob, mastering every sorrow, masking every emotion.

Without any further hope, any desire of ever coming back again, I leave behind the soft, fragile light of dawn that shimmers on the horizon in a blue so pale, so delicately tinged with pink.

The time has come to tear myself away from the last blessed sight of that Mountain, lord of all it surveys, glowing blood-red across the steppe as the sun sets both peak and sky on fire with molten gold.

I hope words will not come crowding hastily in on me; neither pain nor remorse shall deflect them from a course intended to be serene.

To my great surprise, less than a year after the tragedy, I already feel a profound inner peace. But wouldn't Horia herself have wanted me to face the final reckoning like a man, to remain calm when the moment to take leave of the past has finally arrived?

THE COOL DAWN draped in a delicate, almost diaphanous crimson veil. The twilight, all ablaze, covering the Mountain and horizon with a thousand deep red tongues of flame. . . . This dawn, this dusk rent by the muezzin's chant summoning the faithful to prayer, here, in this little village lost in the heart of the vast plain. . . . When with a concentrated effort I try to conjure up the memory of Horia, the images are simple, clear, and powerfully haunting. And no wonder. From the time that we, her children, went off to the city and out into the world, the tempo of her life was determined solely by those two strong beats of the cosmos and of God: sunrise and sunset. This is how I remember her, especially in the summer, when I sometimes managed to return from America for a long-awaited vacation, a few days of happiness at her side.

In the early morning light, Horia is already up and about with the dawn in front of our house, a large, low building of Moorish design decorated with marabout domes and limewashed at the beginning of each summer, so that it glows with a soft whiteness. She bathes her hands and face in the little stream flowing peacefully close to the house, its music a familiar melody amid the immense surrounding silence. Preparing for her prayers, she is all piety and contemplation, yet strangely filled with an almost pagan feeling of contentment. And at that hour, once favored by the lions who roamed the stony, semiarid waste sweeping gracefully and almost flawlessly from our house to the majestic ocher Mountain looming into the sky, one rarely sees another living soul.

IN LATE AFTERNOON, when the intense, exhausting heat of the steppe has finally given way to the triumphant majesty of a miraculous sunset, a twilight filled with the promise of delicious coolness and unparalleled comfort, Horia appears once more before her house. Humbly, she prepares to submit with all her heart and soul to the will of God, yet she still feels stirred by the same singular emotion she first experienced at dawn.

Both morning and evening, at sunrise as at sunset, having discharged her pious duty toward God, Horia sits on her prayer rug and, letting her mind wander freely, leans back against the cool wall of her low white house. With a faraway look in her eyes, lulled by the crystalline music of the tiny brook that relates for her and the distant steppe the epic of the lords of the ocher mountain, and the poem of life, and the passage of time, she sinks into deep meditation, gazing out at the elegant line of the horizon, so clear and unobstructed. Sitting before her home, her kingdom on this earth, she never tires of this marvelous view, like a gift offered to delight a lonely old woman who no longer expects much from this life. She admires that pure and perfect line, so perfect it renders unthinkable the slightest change, which could spoil it. The horizon of Lion Mountain. The Mountain. And what she admires is undoubtedly pride itself, eternity, even though in Horia's heart and mind, there is but one name for eternity: God.

THE HARD WINTER of the plains, with its endless pitch-black nights of bitter cold, has been forgotten. A miracle has occurred. Everyone dreams once more of a breeze, a cool, refreshing breeze.

The human soul no longer huddles in a ball. Horia's being has ceased inventing another life for itself, ceased taking refuge in the bright, warm colors of the kilims she weaves for Little Brother and me, gifts that we may keep or offer to our friends in Paris and New York. Composed of wool that has been laboriously washed, carded, spun, dyed by her hand and hers alone, they are abstract paintings, created each winter to be given away. A thousand geometric patterns of luxuriant shades, abundant love, and overflowing hope, creations that save one from oneself, defying loneliness and even death.

Winter is behind her. So is the prodigious effort the frail old woman expends on the symmetrical arrangement of these delicate and flawless figures, multiplied in breathtaking variations. Their splendor is naive, yet profoundly imbued with exacting necessity. Works of art that owe the beauty of their rigorous composition to an imagination which, at that moment and at each subsequent moment, in absolute concentration and fascination, obeys no other imperative but that of the deflection inspired by a particular blood red, or that of the translation spontaneously suggested by a particular midnight blue, or that of the thematic repetition sprung from the wake of a particular insistent black, or that of the reprise, in parallel or in closure form, dictated by a particular brilliant white. And how could such a prodigious adventure of forms and colors, harmony and correspondence, an adventure subject to such imperious imminent constraints, fail to become the only fate that mattered to Horia during those harsh winter days and nights on the steppe? How could she resist the temptation to withdraw from the world, neglecting everything else in her complete devotion to such a captivating song?

But in these glorious summer hours of dawn and dusk, in these exquisite moments of supreme communion, of deepest happiness, winter has left no trace. Triumphant and expansive, Horia's soul no longer seeks a haven in a kind of artistic paradise. No, the universe itself in all its glory claims her now, takes hold of her completely and carries her off to meet earth and sky, to meet Lion Mountain and the thousand other mountains far beyond, veiled in palest pink or blue.

THESE ARE SONGS that come from far away. Voices that resound across time, across the winding mountain ranges and endless, all-encompassing plains. Murmurs surfacing in the sweet melody of the stream that flows at Horia's feet, in the peaceful silence of dawn or twilight, murmurs that, in the delicate freshness of those moments of utter rapture, tell of the ancestors and their epic journey from long-lost Andalusia.

For this land, this dwelling, that ocher mountain over there, the fine, pure line of that exquisitely beautiful horizon, these peaceful and soothing surroundings, all this has always belonged in its entirety to Horia and her family. It is their sacred property and ancestral birthright, and for as far back as anyone can remember, so it has always been.

FROM HER earliest childhood, Horia had lived with the legend of the noble warrior-lords who fled Andalusia after its reconquest by the Infidel rather than renounce their faith and surrender the ranks and privileges they had earned through their learning and intellectual pursuits. She used to assure us that the very existence of the Mountain on the other side of the stream was proof that the story was true.

HORIA still sees, still hears the galloping cavalcade of riders on the plains, the banners of their clan proudly heading the procession, snapping in the torrid, dusty winds of the vast wastelands hereabouts.

At any time after the first light of dawn, or at twilight, our ancestors might appear in the distance, swarming out of the wilderness beyond the Mountain.

This land is their land; it is their place of refuge and redemption. They claim it for their own, as it claims them in return. It is theirs and always has been.

The tumult of the advancing horsemen grows louder and louder in Horia's mind. A thousand wars, a thousand defeats, a thousand triumphs lie forgotten in their wake; they have scattered the seeds of their knowledge and spirit — as they have their flesh and blood — all the way from distant Gibraltar to this place, on their long journey across the years, across the centuries. The lords of the Mountain, victorious against all adversity, have come. Here they are, and with a deafening roar, the immense, exhausted horde charges for the last time. Appearing on the reddening horizon, they draw closer, pouring down the flanks of the Mountain. This land desires them, calls to them, and they answer.

Land of our ancestors. Ancestors of this arid earth, poor yet so beloved, yes, so beloved by Horia. Ancestors of that venerated Mountain over there.

Source of the time that slips away, and of this stream that flows calmly across the steppe, at dawn and at twilight.

Source of this dwelling where Horia sits, her back against the wall, her tiny body as bent and twisted as an ancient rose laurel in a long-parched wadi, stunted and battered by the burning winds.

The noise of the cavalcade becomes unbearable as it echoes through Horia's head, which, winter and summer alike, is always warmly wrapped in scarves and shawls against the cold and its attendant ills — even against the heat. Always the same image, always the same vision, the same inheritance — the legend of the steppe, faithfully handed down by the carefree little stream. . . .

AND THEN there is the night. Those stifling summer nights, the hot, close atmosphere inside the white rooms, and the inner courtyard, near the little square plots of mint and the jars full of water unrefreshed by the slightest breath of air, giving the lie to the city myth of chilly summer nights on the upland plains.

Horia is outside, leaning back against her house, which is as solid as she, like the weight of centuries. As she sits there in utter darkness, I sense that she is deep in contemplation of the sky, so heavily freighted with its millions of stars. She gazes in wonder at this black roof glittering with gold.

Horia never learned to read or write. But what does it matter, when the starry universe in all its majesty is freely displayed for her admiration and provides the answer to all her questions, in those moments of profound meditation when she is bathed in the silence of the night, caressed by a faint breeze wafting scents of thyme, rosemary, and other delicious perfumes down from the mountains?

A powerful feeling overwhelms her: out there is infinity, beautiful and magnificently organized. We — along with all our ambitions, our triumphs and defeats, our joys and our sorrows, throughout the ages and for all eternity — are but one part in a harmonious whole, the work of a Supreme Being. The angels, prophets, voices of goodness, and messengers of God people the starry sky above us, constantly reminding us of our destiny. The text of the universe written by our Creator is clear and legible; those who sincerely seek the truth have no need to learn anything else. Who (she would ask me), deep down inside himself, does not know his own duty? Who, in the bottom of his heart, does not see where evil lies?

Horia was raised as a child of the steppe. The elders were anxious to protect all those who would one day grow into womanhood from the temptations of the world, of reading and writing, those paths of men which lead to both good and evil. She devoted all her energies to pushing us, her two sons, toward the realm of learning so that we might be worthy heirs to the lords of Lion Mountain . . . and because knowledge, that male preserve, meant not only learning, civility, and manners to Horia, but also — and most importantly — an introduction to sacred things, which in turn further the salvation of the soul.

SHE NEVER ceased reminding us that this earth, this dwelling, this dark and silent vault had been blessed ever since our ancestors, the Ouled El-Gharib, found refuge here in exile from their lost kingdom. They were attracted by the loneliness of the place and the miraculous coolness of the spring gushing from the secret heart of the Mountain. The path is there for us, their children, Horia's children, to follow. When one is descended from such ancestors, when one is the son of such noble lords, of such a land, can one accept any destiny other than that of carrying on so imperious a tradition?

Reading, writing, going out into the world and its cities, New York, Paris . . . Horia would weave her kilims during the cold winter nights, carpets that Little Brother and I would present to others as gifts, but we will never forget. How could we ever forget? We'll tell our friends in New York or Paris that our roots are here. We are the proud sons of this land. We'll bring our French or American friends home with us. Even our golden-haired women, so tall and willowy, will accompany us, and Horia will marvel at their slenderness, at how different they are from the women of this country. They will come with us as well, for that is how our sacred quest for knowledge will end. Horia will welcome these women joyously with a warm heart. But we must always remember what binds us to this land, she would tell us solemnly, because it has been blessed by the lords of the Mountain, whose worthy sons we are, and what does it matter if she, Horia, can neither read nor write. . . .

❖ 5 ❖

I'M WRITING this story for you as well, Little Brother. She loved you best of all. Where are you? Will you ever learn what happened to our mother? Oh, if only we'd been with her when she needed us most!

DESPITE her confidence in our ancestors' promises, Horia couldn't help trembling at the mere mention of your name, for she missed you so much. . . .

The brook's crystal-clear melody, carefree and dreamy, kept us company during the endless night, that vast, dense darkness. We talked about the past, your capricious moods when you were a child, your asthma, all your mischievous exploits — probably undertaken in defiant rebellion against your own frail health — and most of all . . . your *luck*.

"He owes his luck to the learned warrior-lords,"

she assured me with unshakable conviction. "I've prayed so often for them to watch over him. I get up in the middle of the night to remind them of our pact. They are responsible for him. Nothing will happen to him; he's under their protection. He's their son, and he needs their aid. In my dreams they promised to watch over him."

And when all is said and done, that's why Horia never believed that it was purely by chance that, time after time, you kept outwitting death.

"That day when your little brother didn't come home. . . . Do you remember how worried we were, how we waited up all night for him?" she asked me tenderly, her voice low and far away, as though she were speaking only to herself, to the night, and to the little stream. . . . "Darkness was falling, and there was thunder in the air. All the other flocks of Lion Mountain had returned to the village, but there was absolutely no sign of him or of our herd of sheep and goats on the Mountain over there, do you remember?

"I was afraid some misfortune had befallen him . . . a viper . . . a wolf . . . one of those armed bandits who still roamed our mountains despite repeated raids by Monsieur Faure's policemen to keep them from doing any harm. . . . And we waited . . . still hoping, as each terrible minute went by. . . .

"And soon the last rays of the sun had left the earth. . . . Night had fallen, filling the entire universe, save for a few lonely and distant stars. . . . The black silence too, even blacker than the darkness of the grave that will welcome us at our appointed time. . . .

"I'd already sent you to the mosque to warn Imam Sadek. . . . And then you decided on your own to go next to the Spring, the French quarter, braving the terrors of the dark night and the cemetery you had to cross along the way, with your heart pounding. . . . When you reached the Spring, you begged Monsieur Faure to help us, to send his policemen to the Mountain right away to look for my son. . . .

"And that night, even though the poor sainted man was laid up in bed with the kidney ailment that would torment him for the rest of his days, the imam hurried to our house, although he was almost bent double by suffering and barely able to cling to his cane. . . . His face, usually glowing with vigor and health by the grace of God, whom our imam serves with steadfast devotion every moment of the day and night, that face which was normally so elegant and proud, with its magnificent silvery beard which was always kept neatly trimmed, that face was on the contrary deathly pale that night, drained by physical pain and anxiety, because Imam Sadek loved your brother dearly, as everyone else did. And he, more than all the rest of us, could appreciate the boy's lively spirit, exceptional intelligence, and also his pious inclinations. . . .

"But your brother still did not arrive to set our minds at ease, despite all the prayers we offered up together, the imam and I. Monsieur Faure's policemen searched in vain as well, on foot and on horseback, combing the Mountain until dawn, boldly investigating caves, dangerous ravines, steep slopes — may God bless them, wherever they are.

"At dawn we had finally given up hope. We had begun to talk openly of . . . of the will of God.

"And yet I was able to put up a brave front. . . . Yes, I was worried, but never really desperate, when I think about it now. . . . I can even tell you that as the situation began to look more and more catastrophic, I grew strangely calmer . . . more serene, I would say. . . .

"And there was the imam, telling his beads as he kept his crinkly little blue-green eyes fixed upon me, staring intently into my face as though searching for the first sign of my impending collapse. When he realized that I was not going to fall prostrate with grief, he found himself shaking his head gently in astonishment, unless it was in admiration for that remarkable woman — your mother Horia. . . . After all, didn't she seem to be accepting the will of divine Providence with exemplary calmness and humility?

"You and the imam found your mother's silence quite disconcerting, little realizing that while she was serving you coffee — for by now it was morning — Horia was carrying on a passionate silent dialogue with our ancestors . . . reminding them of the pact they had made when your brother had almost died at the age of five from his first attack of asthma. . . .

"Yes, my son: they and I — how could you and the imam have possibly known this? — had agreed that if they would intercede with the Lord on your little brother's behalf, then I would walk to the edge of the desert when summer came — yes, in midsummer, beneath the blazing sun — and bring back some of the incense found only in that particular place, an incense of a uniquely deep and rich perfume, which I would burn in the mosque of our ancestors. And both of us, they as well as I, had faithfully fulfilled our parts of the bargain. . . . They had even contributed more than their share, our ancestors being the men they are, renowned for their generosity and kindness. . . .

"They had seen the wretched state I was in after my third day of penitence beneath the pitiless sun, suffering cruelly from the harsh, jagged stones underfoot, and they had decided to send me a messenger veiled in clouds and dreams, seated majestically on a fiery white Arabian stallion with a flowing mane. . . . In this vision, the messenger promised me — in the name of our ancestors — that your little brother would always, yes, always be protected by the learned warrior-lords. . . .

"But now what has happened? Why has my son not returned with his flock? Has he impulsively indulged a childish whim, a caprice harking back to the time before he was a student at the French school, a time when his afternoons were devoted solely to his pious studies under the imam's tutelage? In those days, he spent his mornings with Saad, who at that time was still our shepherd. Now, bolder than ever, oblivious of fear, he has sent home the One-legged Man, our other servant, and remained alone with the flock. And still we wait for him, although the sun is already up, and the light has overcome darkness, banishing it into oblivion, far away. . . . Perhaps, who knows, in these desperate times when armed bandits roam hungrily. . . . Or else, who knows, a dreadful viper found him as he sheltered from the scorching sun in the shade of a rose-laurel, on the cool white sand of a dry wadi — for although the rumbling skies had threatened to unleash torrents, no cloudburst had soaked the earth below. . . . Yes, who knows, perhaps. . . . But isn't a contract a contract? Deep in my heart, you see, I *knew* that your brother was safe and sound. . . ."

❖6❖

LIKE ALL the other inhabitants of Lion Mountain, and even more than anyone else, Horia's old servant Saad knew what rights this daughter of the Ouled El-Gharib had to her property that stretched — need I remind you? — in a single unobstructed expanse to the Mountain. If Saad will allow himself to be pushed so easily to the brink of tragedy, especially toward the end, it's because in his eyes there is a moment when injustice becomes quite simply intolerable, and there is nothing more unjust than seeing what belongs to you taken away by force. "God does not permit this," he said over and over again to anyone who would listen to him, before he met his violent death at Horia's side. "No one should have to accept this."

❖

I LIKED to listen to his stories on summer nights, when he talked proudly about his adventures during the war, the exploits that had earned him his corporal's pension.

He had only vague memories of all the countries in which he had once fought for France. In fact, for more than five years he had never really understood exactly where he was at all. It was the same universe everywhere, so different from his native village. Wherever he went, he was in the land of the Infidel. The countries were all alike. Huge, rich, verdant fields, slumbering under a sky that was always hopelessly cloudy. The weather was gray or damp, or both, a chilly climate that rarely saw the sun, with its pervasive light and warmth. . . . Wide, straight, endless roads, lines of asphalt that seemed as though they might have been traced with a ruler by the studious and intelligent schoolchildren of Lion Mountain. . . . Houses with sad facades, massive and tall buildings when disaster had passed them by, gigantic displays of thousands of doors and windows exposed to the elements, as though they couldn't decide between life at home and in the street. . . . People who all looked the same with their blue eyes, their wheat-straw hair, men, women, children, everyone bustling about noisily, without any sense of shame or restraint. . . .

And the battles that were Saad's daily lot raged on. A terrible war, terrible in its destruction and debris, shattering noise, and suffering. Death had become the intimate companion of each soldier in the native infantry from the moment they crossed the Mediterranean. . . .

Well then, did it matter what or where France

was? There had been an injustice: that was the main thing. According to Monsieur Faure, the chief of police in Lion Mountain, the Germans had invaded his country. When he heard that, well — Saad's blood just boiled. Was he not the honest son of Nubians who had served the Ouled El-Gharib and their pious, honorable descendants for generations? Monsieur Faure had made no mistake on that point.

"GALLANT sons of this proud village...." It was only yesterday.... Saad could still see the police chief's face, flushed with emotion. They had all been gathered together, about twenty sturdy, well-built lads, in the courtyard of the little school that basked dreamily in the radiant sunshine, bathed in the scents of the Mountain so close by and the lazy buzzing of the bees, intoxicated by spring. It was the first time in his life that Saad had ever set foot there.

FOR MONTHS NOW, at Lion Mountain, they'd been saying that there was a war on . . . probably on some other planet. The villagers didn't consider themselves involved in that sort of thing. They lived a peaceful life. All that mattered to them was to make sure they all had a fair share of the stream's water, which was indispensable to their lives and well-being. War? They didn't know what it was. Apparently it was some kind of calamity that had befallen the Infidels, far away, farther even than the farthest horizon beyond the blue mountains.... "In another world, for God's universe is large," Imam Sadek had assured them during a well-received Friday sermon intended to explain this mystery to his faithful congregation and put an end to useless questions.

"But if the war is some business of the Infidels that is going on way at the back of beyond, why have they come to fetch me, to tear me away from my goats and sheep, my ewes and lambs, my spring farming, and what will Horia think if I abandon all my tasks?"

These are the questions that torment Saad as he watches two mounted policemen come to get him shortly after sunrise, just as he finishes irrigating the last plots of tomatoes. Imperious and insistent, they order him to follow them on foot, without even allowing him to go tell his employer of his departure. Perhaps they're afraid he'll run away.

IN THE COURTYARD of the little school, however, all this changes, in large part due to the expressive countenance of Monsieur Faure, which is at the same time indignant, sincere, and imploring. Holding his kepi in his hands, the chief of police is standing slightly stooped over, quite unlike his habitual erect bearing. He addresses them through an interpreter, of course, for not one of these poor boys has been to school, none of them has the primary school diploma that by colonial decree would have exempted him from military service. Monsieur Faure speaks to them as though he were talking to his own children. Saad senses that he is deeply moved, his voice slightly weary, wounded, the voice of a father who has been profoundly humiliated. This fa-

ther is asking his own people — asking them, these
strong, brave boys — to join forces with him. Avenge
me, wipe away this insult, he seems to cry.

"GALLANT sons of this proud village. . . ." Saad is astonished. He thinks Monsieur Faure could have done without this unbelievable humility, this unusual appeal for
help. Doesn't he have complete authority over the village? If he wants to, isn't it within his power purely and
simply to *command*, as his policemen have just done?
And yet — no. On the contrary: as he lets his eyes,
which are close to tears, wander over Saad and his companions, whom he addresses in a paternal yet tense tone
of voice, he is a defeated man, although he doesn't
admit it openly, someone who in his failure and his sub-
sequently rediscovered humanity is exactly like any
other defeated man, and it is just such a man who asks
these future infantrymen what they would do if someone were forcefully to seize their little patch of ground,
or their house, or anything else that belonged to them.
And that's how the chief of police carried the day.

"YOU, sons or servants of the Ouled El-Gharib, whom
France has always treated with respect! Proud children
of this sacred soil who live in pious awe and devotion!
How would you react if my policemen were to go suddenly berserk and drive you from your homes?"

Saad is the first to reply, saying that he would head
straight for the village's ancestral Mountain. He would
come down again only when he had righted the wrong

31 ❖

done to him. Otherwise he would gladly die up on the Mountain, even welcome the policemen's bullets. They would unlock the gates of paradise for him. . . .

Monsieur Faure now knows, without the slightest doubt, that Saad will make a good soldier.

And Saad will be a good soldier, the bravest in the native infantry, as it turns out.

For five years he will fight in distant, foreign lands, strange lands, but what does it matter? On this glorious spring day, warm and fragrant, standing in the court-yard of this little school, in a village lost in the wilder-ness of the North African steppe, he had sworn to himself that he would fight as well as he possibly could, to avenge — with God's help — this injury to the honor of Monsieur Faure, and from this intensely personal war he will return home a corporal.

He will kill countless Infidels: with a machine gun, which becomes his specialty, his favorite skill, but also with a bayonet, and in hand-to-hand combat. It was a golden opportunity. He kept telling himself that Imam Sadek would approve. He would be at least as grateful to him as Monsieur Faure.

Saad's bravery became legendary.

❖ 7 ❖

THE NUBIAN was the sole villager to return from the war, but he returned with only one leg. He'd lost the other to an artillery shell at Monte Cassino. This name is one of the rare ones Saad can remember distinctly when he tells his stories on a summer night cooled by the breeze from the steppe, while the little stream lulls us with its melody.... For Horia's old farmhand, Monte Cassino had become another word for hell. What he had lived through there had changed him completely. Never again would he be the big cheerful Nubian of old, so playful and whimsical. He had seen the apocalypse up close, as in the worst possible nightmare. He had witnessed the madness of his fellow men — and taken part in it. He had seen torrents of blood flow, and mingled his own in the flood. It was a pensive man who returned to Lion Mountain, a man worried about the future, dubious about the innate wisdom of his fellow man, and convinced that sooner or later, evil would rear its ugly head again. There was no guarantee that the rage which had already seized the world once before, causing such violent upheavals — and costing him, Saad, his leg — would not return. In what form? Where? He had no idea, and in any case, it didn't matter. But before tragedy struck again, it was wise to take precautions, and as Saad grew older, he secretly became more pessimistic, keeping a wary eye out for impending disaster.

I saw less and less of him, for I had gone to America to study, choosing afterward to live in New York, where I opened my first art gallery. I knew, however, that he was watching over Horia, and that he would always watch over her.

IT TOOK him some time to get over the loss of his leg. There was no question of his returning completely to his farming duties, to the great distress of Horia, who wondered how she would ever manage to provide for her family from now on.

Horia had confided her misgivings to Imam Sadek, and one day he summoned the daughter of the Ouled El-Gharib and her devoted servant to his home.

He agrees that the situation is serious. There is no point in blaming the Infidels, however. What is important is to face the problem squarely. With God's help, something can be done.

"And to think that he could have escaped, like so many others," complains Horia, who makes no secret of the fact that she blames Saad for this mess.

"Escape, yes, that's easy to say," replies Saad, who is sitting awkwardly on an old mat spread out in the shadow of the beautiful orange tree on the imam's patio. He is leaning against its trunk, but he can't seem to find a comfortable position, because he hasn't yet become used to his infirmity. His tone is indulgent, however; Saad was speaking mostly to himself, to relieve his own belated doubts, rather than to Horia, for whom he has the most profound and affectionate regard.

The imam maintains an enigmatic silence.

"I, too, was wondering . . ." he remarks suddenly. "But that would have meant going against the will of Providence — and do we have the right to do so? After all, we can never kill too many Infidels. . . ."

The imam falls silent. Then he turns to Saad.

"We owed it to Monsieur Faure, after all, and to his country," he observes. "They treat the clan of the El-Gharib with the greatest respect."

Saad's face brightens. The imam seems to be less harsh with him than Horia is. The Nubian feels the moment has come to break the good news he has been jealously keeping to himself.

"Monsieur Faure told me yesterday that I'll soon begin receiving a disability pension. I'll be a kind of civil servant," he crows triumphantly, breaking into noisy laughter.

Horia is beside herself.

"A civil servant, you? An imbecile who has set foot inside a school only once in his life — and then what for? To get himself sent directly from there out to God knows where, and lose a leg, idiot. You call that being a civil servant. Imam Sadek, do you? Try to talk some sense into this Nubian."

The imam doesn't react. I can still see him, clothed all in white. His neatly trimmed beard is already streaked with ash-gray. His eyes are blue-green. His presence and bearing are radiant with that wisdom which has given him a place in all our hearts and made him the uncontested sage of the village of Lion Mountain, and even of her children far away in Paris or New York.

He reflects awhile, running his long delicate fingers through his beard. Yes, one could say that Saad is now in fact a kind of civil servant. Won't he be regularly receiving money? Horia is going a bit too far. She should show some moderation here, be more careful of what she says. Her two fatherless sons are still quite young. If she's not careful, she might lose this Nubian, and God knows from now on she might need him more than he needs her. Who's going to look after her orchard, her fields, her flock, if Saad — newly rich, thanks to Monsieur Faure — leaves her service? And besides, shouldn't she make an attempt to fathom this miracle? Our Nubian has become a civil servant through having slain so many Infidels. *"It is God himself who repays him thus. . . . "* Imam Sadek states his conclusion in a tone of absolute certainty as he sips his mint tea, seated with his guests in the shade of the orange tree on his patio, surrounded by its gleaming white walls. He turns to Horia.

"Daughter of the Ouled El-Gharib, the Nubians have served our people for generations. Like his ancestors before him, Saad feels only loyalty and veneration for you, for us all. Yesterday he was your shepherd. He also labored in your fields. Your own sons could not have served you better, if they'd been old enough to take charge of your property. Today, it's true, he has only one leg. Let us not forget, however, that he will be receiving a fortune every month — and that is the other leg. . . ."

"The other leg?" interrupts Saad.

"Yes, my son. That one you will rent."

Horia is just as astounded as her servant.

"Really, Imam. . . ."

"I'm telling you that Saad will pay someone to do the work he can no longer perform. Irrigating, for example. But that's not all. . . ."

The imam pauses for a moment before looking up again at Horia, who awaits the verdict she has already accepted. For her, it would be a sacred revelation.

"Horia," intones the imam, "every mystery conceals its own truth. It is the duty of the spirit to make a special effort to seek out this truth. God has so willed. And this is what I have done. From now on, you will go . . . outside. You will join the men of the village. With Saad at your side, you will manage your own property and business affairs, which have suffered more than enough from five years of neglect and abandonment."

FROM THAT day on, thanks to the battles fought by Saad at Monte Cassino and elsewhere, Horia had confronted the world of men, and after they had weathered their initial shock, the men of Lion Mountain had ended by considering her almost like one of them, their equal, since Imam Sadek had so decreed.

FULL OF affectionate admiration for this singular little woman of iron-willed determination, whose intelligence he considered superior to that of many men in the village, Saad would sometimes tease her to help her relax after a particularly hard day, reminding her that he was her liberator. It was thanks to him that she was no longer a prisoner of her own patio. If he hadn't lost his leg at Monte Cassino, she wouldn't be the renowned and formidable Horia, whom no one in Lion Mountain dared challenge.

Horia's reply to the Nubian was unvarying:

"God sometimes does a good job."

Saad wasn't exactly sure what his employer meant by that. Each time he wound up deciding that she still thought he should have headed for the Mountain when Monsieur Faure's policemen came to make a soldier out of him and send him off to fight for France.

THE "OTHER LEG," whose services were acquired thanks to Saad's subsidies from Monsieur Faure's country, and with the blessing of Imam Sadek, was nicknamed "the One-legged Man."

News of the discussions that had taken place at the imam's house to solve Horia's problems had spread like wildfire.

Indeed, there is no such thing as a secret in Lion Mountain. And so Horia's new employee, a slightly retarded young farm worker, was not in the least surprised to hear everyone calling out to him, as he drove his flock through the village for the first time.

"Move along, One-legged Man! Step lively, One-legged Man!"

❖

RUMOR and conjecture had a field day in the village once word of the new trio got around.

How would Horia and her two employees divide up the work among themselves? Which one of the three would be in charge of bringing the year's various seasonal crops to market in Lion Mountain?

Some people had taken unfair advantage of their positions to abuse Horia's trust during the five years when Saad had been given up for dead in foreign lands. Well, now he was back, and he wasn't a ghost. The guilty parties wondered if he might try to take revenge on them.

And Horia herself? Her land has always provided the village with its best tomatoes, its best melons, its best pomegranates, its best figs. All these fruits and vegetables seem to burst with a sweet flavor and sunny aroma unrivaled by produce grown anywhere else on the steppe. And since she is no fool, Horia has seen during the five years she has been imprisoned by tradition within the walls of her home, how unscrupulous middlemen, unconcerned with the salvation of their souls, have been selling off these riches. Thinking only of their own profit, they would rent her fields to sharecroppers for increasingly paltry sums, secretly pocketing commissions that grew fatter and fatter each year. Their dishonesty was revolting, but Horia had no one she could rely on. Imam Sadek needed evidence with which to confront these shady characters, but she was unable to supply any. The imam's only advice, in that case, was that she put her faith in God. Now that he has made her the equal of the village men, everyone in Lion Mountain is afraid. What is she going to do?

❖

THE FIRST crop of tomatoes and pimientos harvested by Horia after Saad's reappearance is an exceptionally good one. The village has hardly ever seen its like, even before the Nubian went off to war.

To foment discord among the trio, spiteful gossips attribute this success to the efforts of the One-legged Man. Saad doesn't mind in the least. He thinks it's rather encouraging that the worker he himself picked out is garnering such praise.

Imam Sadek is of the same opinion. The One-legged Man is a natural phenomenon. He can move mountains, carrying earth and sky together on his big, strong shoulders. He's dull-witted, true, but basically sound. Everything that gratifies his childlike mind and increases his herculean strength is good, thinks the imam. Let them snipe at the Corporal all they want, as long as the Widow and her two fatherless boys reap the benefit.

❖ 9 ❖

MONSIEUR FAURE will be another ally for Horia, as well as a valued adviser. The chief of police hasn't forgotten the sacrifices Saad made for France.

SOON AFTER his return from a prisoner-of-war camp, Monsieur Faure falls into the habit of stopping his jeep in front of Horia's house on his way down from the Spring on Saturdays, when he makes his weekly tour of inspection through the old village.

He honks the horn. Horia hurries out the door carrying a kilim, which she unrolls on the narrow terrace that runs down to the stream.

At first Monsieur Faure stays in his jeep. He simply greets the little woman with a friendly smile.

If Saad is around, he acts as interpreter, for he learned French during the war.

Following the custom of the villagers, Monsieur Faure inquires after Horia's health and business dealings, asking the same question several times.

"And how have you been feeling lately, Horia? Well, I hope?"

"It's kind of you to ask, Monsieur Faure. I'm feeling just fine."

"Feeling well, are you, Horia?"

"Yes, Monsieur Faure, I'm in good health, thank God."

And so forth.

Then they move on to Horia's business affairs, her crops, her flocks of sheep. . . . The conversation continues for some time, a ritual that never changes from one Saturday to the next. Monsieur Faure is a master at this sort of thing and obviously enjoys it immensely.

Every time she hears the horn, Horia dashes for the door with her kilim in her arms, and one Saturday her perseverance pays off: the police chief gets out of his jeep and accepts a glass of mint tea.

It happened on a particularly torrid summer afternoon. The blazing heat was dying down as the huge red ball of the setting sun slipped slowly but inexorably behind the Mountain. It was a passionate and infinitely sad farewell. The entire universe was bathed in a dusty radiance of ocher and blood.

Silently savoring his mint tea as he contemplates the Mountain, Monsieur Faure admires it for the first time in that particular setting, in that moment of splendor, just as Horia will admire it until her tragic end — on her own doorstep.

Monsieur Faure feels overwhelmed by a happiness he has rarely known before this day, a happiness he will wish to reexperience each time he comes here from now on, a singular mixture of contentment, strength, and serenity.

❖ 10 ❖

IN THE VILLAGE, the rumor is that Horia has become powerful.

At first Imam Sadek is disturbed. He doesn't like this gossip about the daughter of the Ouled El-Gharib. And yet, it won't be long before he himself . . . helps spread the rumor. Didn't the Widow go through hard times during the black years when Saad was away? They've got a lot of nerve, those people who complain today about her relations with Monsieur Faure. Didn't they try to ruin her while she kept to her house like a recluse? Alas, even he, Imam Sadek, had been unable to expose the conniving of her enemies and bring this wickedness to an end by denouncing it in his Friday sermons. Well, decides the imam, since those people refused to fear God, let them now fear Monsieur Faure!

❖

ONE DAY, Horia takes advantage of the police chief's visit to proudly show off some of her tomatoes and pimientos. Monsieur Faure is hugely impressed.

"We never see such marvelous tomatoes and pimientos in the village anymore," he remarks to his hostess. "The other crops have been reduced to almost nothing by the plague of migratory locusts that attacked all the fields downstream. You're lucky, Horia. Your lands upstream have all been spared. How do you plan to sell this magnificent crop?"

"We're not quite sure yet," replies Horia. "The One-legged Man will be in charge of the flock. I would like Saad and my older child to go down to the village market each morning with the day's harvest. Thank God," she exclaims, "they won't cheat us ever again!"

"Horia, you seem to me like a person who doesn't need a lot of money," says Monsieur Faure in astonishment.

Horia doesn't understand. How can that be? She has to bring up her two fatherless boys by herself. What is more, she must get ready to send her older son away to boarding school at the end of the summer, to the best lycée in the country, but also, unfortunately, the most expensive. How could she — of all people — not be in need of money? She begins to have doubts about Saad's skill as an interpreter, unless the fool just wasn't listening.

"No, no," insists Saad, "that's exactly what he said. He's reproaching you for wasting your riches."

"Tell him," she says . . . but suddenly falls silent. She has just had a brainstorm. "Tell him," she continues, "that if I had the means of transportation necessary to deliver my produce to other villages as well, even villages on the other side of the blue mountains, we would naturally make even more money. Monsieur Faure is of course aware," she adds, to his amazement, "that the scarcer one makes this or that commodity in each village, the higher the price one will get for it, which is of course perfectly permissible in the eyes of God."

What an extraordinary little woman! thinks Monsieur Faure. That's the very idea he was about to suggest himself: drive prices up by making the merchandise scarce. Except that what he'd had in mind, in the line of transportation, had been simply a few extra mules or donkeys. The Corporal could hunt them up, renting them here and there.

Filled with enthusiasm and respect for Horia's unexpected display of business acumen, Monsieur Faure adjusts his kepi smartly before bowing to his tiny hostess, who is plainly delighted.

Horia won't even need to listen to Saad, who now begins explaining to her that Monsieur Faure would be very happy to have the police van deliver their crop of tomatoes and pimientos to the farthest markets, on the other side of the Mountain — twice a week, if necessary.

THE NUBIAN feels a rush of joy and pride. Isn't this happy turn of events due to him? Isn't it thanks to him that fate has begun to smile on Horia? Every cloud has a silver lining, he tells himself. . . . You never know!

❖ 11 ❖

THE YEAR is 1949, and this July day has been a particularly hot one. Almost 50 degrees centigrade in the shade. It's still boiling hot late in the afternoon, when the heat should already have abated. All the crops are parched and wilted. The plots of melon vines have suffered the most. Saad watches the One-legged Man irrigate that part of the property for the third time since that morning, but his thoughts are elsewhere: what would be the proper way to thank Monsieur Faure for everything he has done for Horia?

THE CHIEF of police is the most powerful man in Lion Mountain, reflects Saad. Surely he has everything. Nothing impresses him.

Should he persuade Horia to invite Monsieur Faure and his wife for lunch at her house?

❖ 48

Saad doubts that his mistress would accept. Since the untimely death of Si Taher, her venerable husband, life has gone out of her household. The dead man's shadow looms everywhere, an imposing presence draped in noble black condemning all to silence and austerity, a state of affairs that wasn't exactly improved by the hardship of the war years.

And then . . . even if she does agree, how will the poor woman carry it off honorably, when times are still difficult, when she's just beginning to emerge from the quagmire into which she sank through the dishonesty of the village's leading citizens? Saad now realizes that they robbed her much more than he'd ever imagined.

Whenever he deigned to respond to their pressing invitations, Monsieur Faure was royally entertained by these same notables in their luxuriously appointed homes. Would Horia be able to match those splendid displays of hospitality so in keeping — it's true, as Saad is quite willing to admit — with the tradition of the Ouled El-Gharib?

Unless she offers Monsieur Faure a superb kilim instead? Hasn't he often expressed his admiration for those magnificent creations that Horia has begun to obtain from her loom?

Or perhaps a richly illuminated ancient manuscript which she would select from among the treasures her ancestors bore safely away with them, so the story goes, in their flight from long-lost Andalusia?

Or else. . . .

❖

AT THAT very instant, the Corporal saw three partridges flying over the crest of the ancient mulberry tree on the property, winging their way toward the Mountain and the spring, doubtless hurrying to claim their share of its refreshing waters before the rest of the crowd arrived.

Then he remembered how the police chief had marveled, during his visits to Si Taher's widow, whenever he saw these birds sailing across the golden sky at the peaceful hour of sunset. They cleaved the air harmoniously, grouped in strictly organized formations, beating their wings so lightly and gracefully that Horia's benefactor readily voiced a longing to caress their russet-gray plumage. The same longing that he, Saad, had felt for the maidens promised to the faithful in paradise. How he would have liked to fondle them, each time Little Brother recited to him the verses of the Koran in which God describes them so imaginatively, so voluptuously!

SUDDENLY the Corporal has a bright idea. He'll ask the One-legged Man to spread a net, as only he knows how, at the very spot where the spring gushes forth from the Mountain, where the birds, gazelles, and a thousand of God's innocent creatures come to quench their thirst early in the morning.

Wiping away the sweat streaming down his brow, the Nubian feels an exquisite coolness blow softly over his face. He smiles contentedly, happy at having come up with an idea he feels sure will meet with Horia's hearty approval.

All this happened just a few years after the war, a war that the people of Lion Mountain had known only through the Corporal's stories.

Even today, more than thirty years later, the One-legged Man assures me that he had never before seen anything like the extraordinary object he came upon while climbing the Mountain at dawn, on his way to the spring to set the trap Saad had ordered him to prepare.

No one in the village, aside from Saad, knew what a tank or a plane was. . . . The war was something that had taken place far away from them, worlds and worlds away from the place where their ancestors, in their wisdom, had put down roots.

No one knew what a machine gun was, either, but that was definitely what the One-legged Man described somewhat confusedly to Saad. The gun had been left in perfect condition, with enough ammunition to withstand a siege of several days, and it was set up at the entrance to a cave overlooking a pass on the other side of the Mountain. Where had it come from? Who had placed it there?

IMAM SADEK and Horia remembered — as did others in the village, including myself, who still remember to this day — having heard explosions in the night, but at a great distance, as in a dream, noises that Saad was to identify as bombardments. Nothing else. We never saw any soldiers on Highway 15, the obvious route for any troops moving up from the south, or any planes in our sky, which remained blue, serene, and reassuring all through that time people called "the war."

We had witnessed no battles, no bloodshed, nothing that might have explained the mystery of that dreadful weapon which burst without warning upon the fragile and diaphanous dawn, in that magical hour of partridges and gazelles, and so threatened to bring evil upon the carefree world of our ocher-walled village, which up until that moment had lain drowsing peacefully in the midst of the vast North African steppe.

II
Lightning

❖ 12 ❖

"THE TIME had come for the French to leave, and they left. Just as the learned warrior-lords, in olden days, had left Andalusia when their time had come as well. That is the way of the world, that is the way the wheel of fortune turns, down through the centuries: victors one day, vanquished the next. There is no glory in that, my son. No shame, either. So much the better if fate smiles on us today. But let us remember that the river of time bears away the bitter tears of the conquered as well as the joyous celebrations of the conquerors, drowning all in nothingness and oblivion. Only God is great."

"How well you speak, Horia! Such a way with words! You'll never cease to astonish me!"

"He who fears not God today shall face the consequences tomorrow. Nothing is erased from the tablets of the Lord."

"That's right. Go explain that to the Delegate, he'll listen to you. You really think he cares a fig for the Lord?"

"What does it matter if he listens to me or not, Nubian! The truth is still the truth. Even the Delegate can't claim to have the last word where truth and justice are concerned. Stop contradicting me, you wretched creature!"

"You'll never change, Horia! You cling stubbornly to your illusions, and unfortunately that's all they are, your stories about truth, justice, and everything else. I'm telling you again that this government, this political party, this country, this Delegate, these people aren't afraid of anything, and certainly not of your 'Lord' — whom I respect, let me hasten to add. But you must understand that we've now entered a time of tyranny. Whoever refuses to submit must beware! Do you know what they'll do to him?"

SAAD shows me the cigarette burns on his arms. When he takes off his shirt, I can see stripes of a septic blue, mottled with blood, left by the blows of a truncheon on his back. He tells me about his three months of torture. How he spent an entire week without food or water in a dank, coal-black cellar infested with rats and flooded with water, the basement of a dilapidated building in a big city, perhaps the capital. How he was kept standing for seven whole days — him, a cripple, and almost naked — under the watchful eye of a sadistic jailer. Yes, three months of hell from which he emerged with his hair turned prematurely white. "Frankly," he tells me, with a slight pout of disdain, "it made Monte Cassino seem like a picnic."

But he himself is still the same man I've always known, as resolute and defiant as ever. Recovering his self-control, he turns to Horia: "I will never, ever, become a member of the Party and accept their card, even if it costs me my life."

Horia remains impassive. All three of us are sitting on an antique kilim in the shade of the western wall of our limewashed patio, which gleams whitely in the early morning light. The day is still young, in that summer of 1958, and the cool oasis at the foot of the wall is spacious and vibrant.

Although Horia will soon be sixty years old, her complexion, weathered by the sun and the dry winds of the steppe, makes her seem strangely youthful and vigorous. I find her preoccupied, however, and somewhat tired, especially around the eyes. She no longer smiles as readily and joyously as she once did, in spite of the thousand and one difficulties of everyday life.

OUR SILENCE is prolonged and heavy. I imagine the torture endured by Saad. His resistance to pain was proverbial, rumored to be almost unequalled. People said that at Monte Cassino he'd continued to man his machine gun even after the enemy shell had torn off his right leg. He'd promised to do his best, so he kept on fighting: it was as simple as that. When the Party's henchmen tried to break his spirit, what was the only thing left for them to try? Humiliation! They forced him to drink his urine and smeared his face with his own excrement.

When I look at that handsome face now, at those comely features carved in ebony and marked with the same dignity that distinguishes the man, so profoundly good, honest, and proud, I glimpse a tear just starting to roll down his cheek, and it breaks my heart.

Horia senses my sorrow and regret.

"There was nothing you could have done in any case," she tells me. "Neither you nor anyone else. You have nothing to blame yourself for. What good would it do?"

"All the same, Horia!" I reply, trying in vain to control my anger. "I would have come immediately, if only I'd known."

"What could you have done against such tyranny? Nothing. It simply had to run its course, as fate decreed."

And staring reproachfully at Saad, she added, "He promised me he wouldn't tell a soul about this, not even the imam, and especially not you. But unfortunately what I feared has come to pass. This Nubian has sown uneasiness in my son's mind just when important examinations await him, only weeks away."

THE DELEGATE, the new authorities' very first representative in Lion Mountain, wanted to enroll all adult males in the Party. The portrait Saad draws of him is hardly flattering. A short, slightly built young man, it seems. His forehead is low and narrow. He has a thin mustache. Like one of those circumflex accents Little Brother used to pen so neatly but with too much ink when he was still at school, the mustache sits upon a dry and bony face deeply pitted by smallpox. Petty malevolence made flesh and blood.

And the man appears to be very full of himself. Always sprucely turned out, with a perpetually dashing air. He invariably wears a three-piece suit of shiny black material. It seems that from the first day, nobody was left in any doubt at all about the man's colossal self-importance, arrogance, and conceit, which he shows off at the wheel of a luxurious black Citroën, driving with ostentation and contempt through the narrow, stony streets of our poor little village at breakneck speed, making an incredible racket and leaving behind great clouds of dust.

As soon as he took charge of the Delegation, which had remained unoccupied for more than a year, our little village tyrant, who thirsted for influence and authority, selected — out of all the possible candidates to fill the office of public crier — Horia's retarded farmhand. Who would ever have imagined it?

And so from dawn to dusk for three days running, the Simpleton shouted his lungs out in every corner of Lion Mountain: in the Spring, our former French quarter; in the old village, from house to house and in front of every street stall; even at the doors of the mosque, as well as for the benefit of the ruminating camels in the livestock market, the exhausted mules and donkeys brutalized by the heat and human stupidity, assorted skeletal stray dogs, and the cackling chickens roaming freely over Highway 15 as it lay dreaming in the spring sunshine.

And what tidings did this inspired messenger bring? That the Party was the Motherland. That everyone should prove his great worth by acquiring a Party card — upon payment of a certain sum, of course. And no holdouts, or else! Recalcitrants risked losing their share of irrigation water. Close scrutiny would unmask the guilty ones.

Since what was at stake was the life or death of their crops and tiny plots of land, the source of all well-being for them and theirs, all male adults had felt they had no other choice but to accept their fate and trudge off, one by one, heads bowed in resignation, to the former police station now serving as headquarters for the new authorities.

Horia's property was upstream, however, and too close to the spring to risk being deprived of its fair share of water. Following the example of the other villagers, and just to be on the safe side, Saad had nevertheless thought it wise to ask Imam Sadek for his advice. The latter, after careful consideration, had confirmed the Nubian's original opinion. No, Horia and Saad weren't at risk, that was quite true. Still, it was better to be practical, after all, and cooperate with the authorities. In a word, to avoid unnecessary complications, the imam had advised against causing any trouble, because he, too, was beginning to be apprehensive about the future.

As always, however, Saad will end up doing exactly as he pleases. As always, he'll insist on seeing things only in their simplest, most essential light. And to get to the heart of a problem, he had decided there was only one way to go.

His reasoning was crystal clear. The house isn't on fire, he told himself. The village is in no danger, right? Now, he, Saad, learned all he needs to know about danger at Monte Cassino. No one, and certainly not that scarecrow of a petty tyrant at the Delegation, has to cry danger while waving a Party card under his nose. If Horia, if Imam Sadek, or the Ouled El-Gharib clan were threatened, then, yes, it would be understandable. In which case, plenty of people can vouch for the Corporal's courage. Everyone knows what he can do. Even though he has only one leg left, through the fault of the Infidels, nobody doubts that if he had to, he would not hesitate to take up a weapon. Even . . . to take the machine gun from its hiding place under the ancient mulberry tree, the same gun the Simpleton discovered one day while chasing around after partridges, and which has been kept in perfect shape, unbeknownst to anyone, not even Horia, thanks to his secret but constant attention. No, really, decided the Nubian, the house is not on fire. Thank the Party anyway for having thought of him. And thanks also to Monsieur the Delegate and Madame the Motherland. It's very nice, all that, but really, no thanks.

"YES," nods Horia, as our oasis of shade shrinks inexorably beneath the assault of sun and heat upon the patio, prey now to the merciless fire, "everything that Saad has told you is true, and that's how the rumor quickly spread that no one had seen the Nubian stop by the Delegation to pledge allegiance as the others had done and pick up his card.

"I thought immediately that it must have been one of those charitable souls, those distinguished citizens who had never forgiven me for having managed to send you to study in America, to seek learning and excellence so far away, following our ancestors' precepts — and for preparing to send your little brother away to Paris for the same reasons. And how had I succeeded in achieving all this? Only by the sweat of my brow. Not by stealing or killing. No, solely through the hard work of the Nubian, the Simpleton, and your old mother. Yes, I ask you: who else, if not one of those creatures consumed both night and day by envy?

"In short, some coward denounced our Saad and committed that terrible evil without a moment's thought for the wrath of God. But that's the way some people are: they cannot bear to see their fellow men find contentment and — why not? — happiness through toil and fear of the Lord.

"The Delegate was also told that I myself was a woman who cared little for the codes of honor. That I would scoff at the traditions of my ancestors. Outside the walls of my house, I would bustle about shamelessly, tirelessly. My face unveiled, my head held high, I would mix with other men like a man. I'd struggle without respite at their sides, and sometimes — even often, and tenaciously — against them. But do they still not understand, those people, that I was fighting to keep from being trampled underfoot? What can they be thinking of? Without my efforts, my fatherless boys would have perished long ago.

"Yes, those wicked tongues spread so many nasty lies about us, and why? For the sole purpose of causing us harm.

"One night, late in the spring, Saad disappeared. He didn't come home. Saad and the Simpleton had left together early that morning to irrigate the crops, and I waited for the two of them that evening, anxious and impatient. The Simpleton returned, but he was alone, and unable to tell me anything about the Nubian. I stayed up all night long, waiting for him.

"I didn't see him again until barely two weeks ago, and he was in the same state you find him now. But God is our refuge and our sole resource, for He does not forget."

❖13❖

IMAM SADEK had learned that I'd returned from America on vacation. That afternoon, as on every similar occasion for the last three years, he did not wait for me to go pay my respects to him in his own home but came directly to our house.

The mingled aromas of chewing tobacco and rare, exquisite scents that emanated from his person, his bearing, everything about him seems to proclaim his arrival from afar. Even before he reaches our front gate, his presence, his aura, slowly fill our home. The same miracle occurs anew. Space and time are fused in the precise instant when we glimpse the imam's face, radiant with splendor and authority, through our half-open front door. That moment is perfumed, once again, by the fragrances of mint and jasmine wafted through the evanescent air on this late afternoon by the little pleasure garden on the patio, which Horia herself has

freshly watered, as she does each day after the wither-
ing heat of summer has died down with the approach
of dusk. And so this moment becomes, once again and
for all eternity, the moment in which the imam ap-
proaches with open arms and a reassuring smile on his
lips, as I wait to welcome him happily, deeply moved
by the strength and warmth of the affection and veneration I feel for him.

"AH, OUR SCHOLAR! Our dear scholar! May God bless
you, my son! Here you are, back again. You have no idea
how much we've missed you!"
　　"I've missed you, too, Imam. I've missed you all
very much."
　　"How have you been? Well, I hope?"
　　"Quite well, Imam. I'm in good health. And how
have you been?"
　　"Oh, all in all, I'm doing fine. We shouldn't complain. And your studies, my son? How long will it be
before we welcome you home a doctor?"

AS FAR as the imam was concerned, there was only one
reason to go so far away, all the way to America — yes,
to *America!* Almost to another planet! — and that was
to become a *"doctor."* To the imam, to Horia, indeed to
everyone in Lion Mountain, that word was a vague but
magical title that commanded respect. The bearer was
assumed to possess all sorts of qualifications, including those of a physician, an engineer, a professor, and a
man endowed with natural gifts of authority. In other

words, an imposing constellation of knowledge and power. And since America was so far away, almost at the ends of the earth, the imam and his faithful flock imagined that any accomplishments acquired there must necessarily be among the rarest, the most worthy of admiration. Otherwise, if one intended to return from America as anything less than a *doctor*, then why not simply stay in Lion Mountain? Why bother to go off and suffer so far away, why risk dying of homesickness when one can stay in the village, nourishing one's soul and mind on the traditions of learning and saintliness handed down by the lords of the ocher mountain?

"Ah, our dear scholar, may God bless you, Doctor! May the ancestors bless you, my son!"

"YES, IMAM, pray for him," calls out Horia, who joins in the conversation from the kitchen, where she is busy preparing . . . *coffee*, because at this hour of the day, according to some mysterious calculation known only to herself, Horia has concluded that the imam drinks only . . . *coffee*, "*and not mint tea, which he drinks the rest of the time, except early in the morning, naturally.*"

Naturally. And she will flavor this coffee, prepared especially for the imam, with rose water. "*Naturally*," once again, it seems that this is how the imam likes his coffee: delicately flavored with rose water. Each time he drinks it he never fails to remark, with the same hint of secret reproach:

"Rose water again, daughter of the Ouled El-Gharib!"

And each time Horia replies, with complete complicity:

"But really, you know very well that's how you like your coffee, Imam Sadek!"

The imam says nothing. He sips, he savors.

As for me, I looked on, and remained silent as well. I didn't try to understand. I gazed in admiration. I knew that their complicity was perfect.

THAT AFTERNOON, contrary to her usual custom, Horia had been in a great hurry to come and join our conversation.

The imam and I are now seated near the beds of mint, under the big apricot tree on the patio.

I could see the haste written on Horia's face, in her eyes, as she came toward us: small, delicate, fragile, bearing the coffee service on a tray of walnut wood that trembled in her hands.

Whenever I'd come home to Lion Mountain in the past, on all the other occasions when Imam Sadek had arrived to greet me, Horia had disappeared for a long while out in the kitchen, apparently in order to allow the imam and me ample time to ourselves for our many hugs and repeated exchanges, the "How have you been?" and "Quite well, thank you," the imam's "Ah, our dear scholar, may God bless you, my son!" and all the rest of our happy little ritual that I so cherished.

The strange thing is, you see, that the imam, even while he was still here with us on this earth, was in Horia's eyes some sort of saint. Actually, he *was* a saint.

As far as Horia was concerned, the proof was readily available to anyone who bothered to take the time to reflect upon the wisdom that flowed from his person and the "miraculous" actions he would sometimes perform. This being the case, what could Horia possibly desire for her son upon his return from faraway America, a country, moreover, which probably didn't offer much in the way of saintliness or miracles? What might she desire for her son? Obviously, more than anything else in the world, she wanted to see him immersed once more in the wisdom and holiness of his ancestral village. Immediately, deeply immersed, without the slightest distraction by any third person, not even Horia.

Oddly, however, on this particular afternoon, when she hurries in to us with her tray of piping-hot rosewater coffee, I have the distinct impression that she'd rather not leave me alone with the imam for very long. Indeed, Horia seems anxious to stay close to us, as though she feels that her presence, unfortunately, is of such importance that it temporarily eclipses all considerations of wisdom, saintliness, and miracles.

It was clear that Horia quite simply did not want me to have a chance to speak privately with the imam.

Could she be afraid that I might break the promise I'd made that morning? Does she think that her presence will force me to be silent, that I'll keep quiet regarding those matters we decided to keep secret from the imam, at least for the time being? Out in the kitchen, did she remember how hard it had been for me to control my rage this morning, as we sat out by the west wall, and did she wonder if I'd be able to keep from bursting out angrily with the truth if I found myself alone with the imam?

Yes, very likely. Quite probably, in fact. I saw the worry in her face. I read it in the look she gave me when our eyes met as she emerged from the kitchen carrying the imam's coffee, delicately flavored with rose water.

❖ 14 ❖

MORE THAN fifteen years have now gone by since that day, and yet, I can still see everything, smell everything, hear everything. Or was it only yesterday?

Was it yesterday, the unique aroma of that coffee, the scents of mint, jasmine, and sweet-smelling tobacco, all mingling in the fragrant air?

Was it yesterday, that late afternoon, so light, so enchanted, when the limpid atmosphere seemed to tremble as the sky became suffused with a purple glow?

Was it yesterday, the feeling of well-being experienced in that moment of respite, in the freshly watered little patio garden, after the blazing noonday heat?

Was it yesterday, the affectionate but determined look with which Horia hoped to remind me of my promise, made earlier that morning?

Was it yesterday, the slow, deliberate, resonant voice of Imam Sadek?

Was it only yesterday, the past?

EACH OF US carries with him, among his resources in life's struggle, a few deeply engraved images from his early years. They come — usually at their own bidding — to remind us of the many twists and turns in the long road already traveled. These images are beacons of light, safeguarding for all eternity those precious moments and loved ones we have lost, those parts of ourselves we treasure in secret, the better to preserve them from the banality of everyday life. The sorrowful or joyous events recounted in this narrative belong to this luminous heritage.

I CAN still hear, as though it were yesterday, Horia's soft, melodious voice that morning, in the shade of the western wall of the patio. The two of us are talking. Saad has fallen asleep. Patiently, stubbornly, without ever losing her temper, she tries to convince me, to explain to me why we should not inform Imam Sadek of the horrible punishment inflicted on Saad for his refusal to accept the Party card.

"It would be useless."

"You, Horia, you say this?"

"Evil always destroys itself."

"Really!" I exclaim. "You ought to practice what you preach. You fight back, though, don't you? And refuse to leave your enemies in peace? You admit it, right?"

"I repeat," she insists confidently, "that everything that is totally and basically corrupt is irrevocably doomed to perish. Of its own accord. Why interfere from outside? There's no need."

"Horia, your argument is truly indefensible. Let's suppose that Imam Sadek is not told about this. Therefore, he does nothing. He does not denounce these outrages today. What will happen tomorrow? It will be the others' turn. Your turn, perhaps — who knows? Is that what you want?"

"The others? Don't be silly! They're sheep. . . . They all swear by the Delegate now."

"Exactly, because there's no alternative. No other recourse. Like the imam."

"That's what you think! They're cowards, believe me."

"Look at Saad," I say. "Where did his courage get him? Did you see the state he's in? And how can you be certain it will stop there? He'll say, 'No, no card.' They'll say, 'Oh yes. Or else the cellar, the beatings, and the rats.' So you see, there's not much chance that this evil will destroy itself. It might even triumph. Unless Imam Sadek does something. Quickly, now. Otherwise, I won't be able to go back to America at peace with myself."

"Precisely. . . ."

"What?"

"I have only the two of you in this life. Your little brother and you. You will still have to return here. To this village. To this country. So, a reckless move . . .

well-intentioned, but imprudent. Why provoke the Devil? Just imagine the consequences. . . . Better let the Devil destroy himself."

"Where's the provocation?" I ask. "And how are Little Brother and I . . . "

She interrupts me: "No more, my son. I pray to the Lord night and day, asking Him to spare you all suffering."

"And Saad? What about his mangled back? The cigarette burns? The humiliation? Isn't that horrible? Come on! Saad is my brother, my father, my friend. He's as dear to me as you are, Horia, as dear as Little Brother. This Delegate, these criminals all deserve to hang. And you, you talk to me about being rash, about provocation? What would have become of you, of us, if you hadn't decided to fight? Without your veil. In public. The powerful villagers were plotting against you, when we were still little, but you didn't hesitate to confront them. Did you take up their challenge, yes or no? You didn't wait calmly on your patio with your arms crossed, waiting for evil to destroy itself. No, no, I insist. We must alert the imam right away. Absolutely. Today. Tell him everything. We'll see what his reaction will be."

"I know what his reaction will be."

"Tell me."

"That's just it. That's why I'm begging you to say nothing. You'll only be here for a few days. I beg you to keep quiet during those few days."

❖

I'M DUMBFOUNDED. I don't recognize Horia anymore. Or am I somehow failing to grasp the true dimensions of the situation?

I'd left the village so many years before. Boarding school. After that, America. I'd come back during the summer. One or two weeks of vacation. I was becoming a stranger to the deeper current of village life. Only my childhood memories endured. The rest was fading away, vanishing irretrievably — indeed, had slipped beyond my grasp a long time ago. Horia sent me news in her letters; she scurried here and there, trotting after this person or that one, trying to wheedle someone into writing letters for her, and thanks to these letters I remained in contact as well as I could. And on every vacation I renewed my ties to home by listening to Horia's stories on the long summer nights. With the melodious brook murmuring in the background, she would tell me of the latest torrential rains, the most recent sandstorms, and the thousand other events both great and small that had befallen our village, which nonetheless went on imperturbably, like the Mountain after which it was named. The essential bond was lost, however; the village I had left behind had abandoned me in turn. From that moment on I was an exile. A stranger. Was it so surprising that I should now be unable to understand what Horia was trying to explain to me? Was I right to blame myself for not understanding?

Yes, she thought what had happened to Saad was revolting. Yes, such horrible despotism should not be tolerated. Yes, she suffered for Saad just as much as I was suffering for him. . . . But there, right there, it was at that precise point in her reasoning that I lost her. I couldn't follow her argument when she begged me not to say anything. There was obviously a link missing here in the chain of her logic, if that's what it was.

It's this missing link that Horia will finally reveal to me, after a heavy sigh filled with all the worry in the world and all the love a mother is capable of feeling for her child.

Saad had awakened in the meantime and gone out, leaning painfully on his crutches, to buy what we needed for dinner and the probable — no, certain — visit of Imam Sadek in the afternoon.

Horia poured out her heart.

"Whenever an epidemic, a plague of insects or grasshoppers, or a burning wind, or some other nameless calamity has struck us, this village has always bowed before the onslaught. It has given death and misfortune their due, and then death and misfortune have run their course. The air has become once more that dry, pure, healthy air we breathe, the sky has clothed itself again in that most glorious blue we love to gaze upon, the Mountain over there has bedecked itself in its most beautiful blood-reds, which we have always — young and old, men and women — so enjoyed admiring, and each time life has returned to itself once again. We struggle, every one of us. And everyone in this village — that's how it is, my son — has always known what is important and what is not, what can be tolerated and what cannot, how to go on living in spite of hardship and even how, sometimes, to find a bit of joy in this treacherous existence. Everyone knows this: Saad, your mother, the others. All of us, we all know. We fall down, we pick ourselves up. We fall again, we get up again. This has been going on for centuries, in the shelter of the Mountain over there. You, you went away. Your little brother will leave one day. I would not want any evil to befall us as long as I still have you, your studies, your happiness to think of.

"Saad agrees with me. Yes, he endured injustice. Yes, he suffered. But God is here. And this Delegate won't last forever. Nothing lasts forever. They'll forget Saad, Saad will forget them, them and their tyranny, and things will be as they were, believe me. Another test of adversity, that's all. It will turn out to have been nothing more. As for justice against those who hurt Saad so badly, the Lord will take care of that. They'll perish for having inflicted unthinkable suffering on their fellow man, because what they did to Saad is terrible indeed. It's the very heart of their humanity that is corrupt. Let's leave God to carry out his will in his own domain. Saad will forget.

"Nobody in the village knows what happened to him when he disappeared. I told everyone who asked about him, even the imam, that Saad was ill. I told them that's why no one had seen him for three months. The Simpleton said the same thing. My son, in the face of such inconceivable evil, so much horror, silence is the only worthy human response. Don't worry, life will return to normal. Forgetfulness is the cure for horror. And then one day you — and your little brother, too — will be on top of the world, with the future all spread out before you. When that time comes I'll be very old, with all my worrying about you over and done with, and the Nubian will be an old man as well, with not a single memory left of the tortures he endured. A test of adversity, like a thousand others. Suffered in silence. We fall down, we get up again, and life goes on, in silence. Why bring the imam into this? He'll speak out about it, there'll be complications, and God only knows what might happen then. Who knows what this Delegate and these people off in the capital are capable of doing? We must pray to the Lord for his protection. We must pray to the Lord. You're all I have, my son, and I feel old age coming on. Promise me you'll say nothing. . . ."

HER VOICE was choking with emotion, barely audible toward the end. Yet I can still hear Horia as though it were yesterday: frail, pleading. I see her beautiful face, the delicate features chiseled by time, by the sun and the steppe, already marked by life. I see her eyes filled with tears of anguish. As though it were yesterday. And I can still see with absolute clarity, the blazing, blinding whiteness of the limewashed wall before us, drenched in sunlight.

I had promised.
I had given my word.

And late on the afternoon of that same day, when Imam Sadek came to welcome me home with our joyous, cherished ritual of affectionate and respectful embraces, I said nothing. Not because Horia had hurried to come join us, no, not at all. I said nothing about Saad's ordeal because I had given my word.

And I had given my word because I had understood.

❖ 15 ❖

I HAD returned to America, and come home again the following summer.

I HAD waited for this vacation with even more impatience than usual. I had missed them all, especially Saad.

Homesickness aggravated by a bad conscience, that vague sense of guilt we often feel when we blame ourselves for perhaps not having done enough to ensure the happiness of those we love, from whom life has separated us.

Throughout that whole year in America, I had been haunted by Saad's tragedy. At times I'd been close to despair.

Because of what had happened, and the secret I had carried inside me ever since, I had become someone who felt like an outcast. As though I suffered from a shameful illness. Something inconceivable, as Horia had said. There was something profoundly ugly about the whole affair. Saad's stories of what had happened in prison filled me with disgust, a revulsion that would come over me at the most unexpected moments, stronger and all the more frightening because I had kept the secret to myself.

I would rather have disappeared forever, without a trace — I would rather have died than reveal the cause of my torment to my fellow students, who thought so highly of me.

Lion Mountain itself was already the great secret of my life, a secret that remained entirely separate from the orderly, rational life I led with my companions, as someone passionately engaged in the sacred pursuit of learning Horia had so desired for her sons. This secret was my magic world; I lived it apart from the real world, and I considered it my right to do so even with friends who loved me. And I lived this secret as though it were a privilege. Lion Mountain was my secret garden. I was secretly proud of it. It was that pride I had lost when I was forced to harbor the other secret. My nights were often filled with bad dreams.

HORIA said nothing to me in her letters, which others had written for her, but practiced forgetfulness instead. Time passes; pain is forgotten, horror is forgotten. Only by remaining silent in the face of horror may we escape it. Water still flows in the little stream; the ocher mountain defies time, wreathing itself in its blood-red veils every day at sunset. All is peace, all is happiness — or rather, more often, contentment — and our troubles are forgotten. Why bring up the pain again by talking about it, deliberately reviving it with our words? Why hurt *ourselves* this time? No — let's forget it. The only cure is silence. And so there was not one word in her letters about what had happened the previous summer.

Throughout that entire year, however, despite my anguish, my fits of disgust, my nightmares, I would sometimes begin to hope. Horia would turn out to be right. When I saw them all again that coming summer, everything would be as it had been before, through the miraculous intervention of time, forgetfulness, and the ancestors. Lion Mountain would have recovered from the unthinkable. Saad's handsome face, and his proud, manly bearing would have rid themselves forever of that shame which clung to him like an unspeakable memory, and Horia would no longer need to beg me to remain silent.

THE BUS that I had taken, as I did every year the day after my arrival in the country by plane, let me off at Lion Mountain after a long and exhausting trip along Highway 15.

The village is still the same, drenched in molten sunlight at this, the hottest hour of the day, the hour of fire, which is also the hour of emptiness, repose, and silence.

Not a soul stirs in this vast expanse, sovereign and solitary, bounded only by the Mountain that faces Horia's house, off in the distance.

The air crackles; nothing moves. The light is blindingly harsh. Everything glints and glitters. The entire universe is aflame, dazed, torpid.

Even the old village, which lies a little way off and downhill from the highway, and which at other times during the day is so green, so cool and pleasant to the eye, particularly in the morning, has disappeared beneath an orange cloud of ocher dust and burning sun, while further on mirages of a thousand colors lead the eye on to an infinity of fire that vanishes over the horizon.

Yes, fire is everywhere, and solitude, as they always are at this hour. But Horia's house is there. I saw it.

IN THE PAST, Saad and the Simpleton would wait for me, as they did last summer, under the poplar where the bus always stops.

They'd leave Horia back at the house, "at the front," nervous, happy, impossible, busy in her kitchen reverently preparing for that glorious moment, the most highly anticipated moment of the year. The two men would be the first to greet me, the first messengers of peace and happiness from Lion Mountain.

As soon as he caught sight of me getting off the bus, Saad would be ready to burst out laughing. Despite all he had gone through, a sheer joy seemed to remain his only way of expressing himself. As for the Simpleton, he'd always pounce on whatever luggage he thought likely to be mine, hurrying to grab everything before Saad could lend a hand. I never failed to enjoy this inevitable performance, and so, in spite of the heat and my fatigue, I would find happiness again, and know that even greater happiness awaited me at home.

THAT SUMMER, when the door of the old bus finally opened and I began to climb down its wobbly steps, I saw only the Simpleton's huge frame looming up before me. Saad was not there. Even more surprising and disquieting was the Simpleton's complete inability to give me any coherent explanation for Saad's absence.

❖ 16 ❖

"THAT'S THE way it is. But why us? This poor black man? And must evil go about like that, disguised with such honeyed smiles? Such treachery? Ah, my son, that Delegate. . . ."

HE HAD formed the habit of stopping in front of Horia's house, and since he was the Delegate, and since Horia was born with hospitality in her blood, she would open the door to invite him in to drink mint tea or coffee, and he, the Delegate, the short young man, so slender and dapper, with the pencil mustache like a circumflex accent, and the thin, pockmarked face, this Party henchman, would enter, quivering with affability, unctuously attentive, all smiles — forced smiles — for his hostess. Hypocrisy itself.

❖

"GOD DID not teach me how to see into the hearts of his creatures. What would become of us? Where would that lead us, if we had to fathom the secrets that lie hidden behind each face? No, no. Each of us is alone responsible for his intentions, for what he conceals within his soul. If God had wanted evil to be legible, given openly to be read by everyone, He would surely have written it clearly on every face, and your mother would not have had any trouble seeing the unwholesome reality behind the smiles, the solicitude, the seeming desire to please, and so many comings and goings: the simple, brutal, continuing determination to do harm. Yes, to harm Saad, who would not submit. But that's how it is. God in his wisdom did not grant me this power, and He is right. He puts us to the test.

"Your mother's period of trial has been a long one. All last winter and spring.

"I hear the Citroën's horn, a loud, insistent noise. I go out to open the courtyard gate. There he is, with the same venomous smile, the same effusive and insincere courtesies — and I assure you that he's very good at that game. I invite him to come in. He comes in. He sits down. Always obsequious, he asks after my health, my business affairs. As a crowning piece of infamy, he asks after the Nubian's health as well.

"And each time he tells us about a new episode in what he proudly calls the 'epic of the Party,' or about another miracle by the man he calls, in a voice trembling with veneration, 'Monsieur the President,' who has returned in triumph to the country by way of the sea, on a white horse — or so he claims — like a prophet. A new prophet for these strange times of ours, I tell you.

"Saad and I would listen in amazement. He'd rattle on. And what talent he had! Each time, a new episode, a new miracle. This president who sprang out of the sea one day on a white horse.... Well, we wondered....

"I'd serve coffee or mint tea, depending on what time of day it was, for by this time I knew the habits and tastes of this son of Satan. And he, he never tired of praising his president, and the struggles of 'Monsieur the President,' his supreme sacrifices for the nation, his glorious victories and his far-reaching vision, his goodness and power, his magnanimity, his innate generosity, and his acute sense of duty. Tireless, I'm telling you, this Devil's spawn. As for us, we'd be openmouthed, all ears. We weren't going to ask any indiscreet questions, after all, or embarrass our guest with untimely remarks — the rules of hospitality forbade it.

"At night, however, around the embers of our fire, we were bursting with questions. Saad most of all. He was still suffering a bit from his wounds and burns and he wondered.... He warned me not to believe everything I heard. Only the Simpleton wanted to meet 'Monsieur the President,' that archangel of the clouds who'd sprung suddenly from the waves riding a spotless white horse. Our Simpleton would have fits of laughter, ecstatic laughter, foaming at the mouth, his eyes gleaming with an inspired light. A full-fledged trance. But Saad, you know him: always his own man.

"The Delegate would tell us other things about his president. He assured us he was president of the entire country and therefore desired the happiness of Lion Mountain, the joy and contentment of each one of us, even though, as everyone knows, Lion Mountain is cut off from everything, an impoverished village set down in the middle of nowhere by the Lord and our ancestors, with — can you imagine — this one blacktop road passing through, forever deserted. Nevertheless, 'Monsieur the President' wants our village to be happy, thinks of us constantly, sometimes day and night, even going without sleep, according to the Delegate. Oh, that fiend!

"And this president knows each one of us in Lion Mountain, because in this village, each man is his son, each woman his daughter. And he worries. He came from the sea, he returned to the country — the Motherland — through the gateway of the sea. And why? So that he could worry, and his hair has already turned white from anxiety. We're all his sons and daughters, he says. . . . But what does he know about it? Stranded as we are out in the middle of nowhere . . . desert, rocks, desolation, and the burning sun . . . just a little stream flowing bravely, our earthly Paradise, which we owe to God and the ancestors.

"No matter. We listened, Saad and I, even though we began to have serious doubts at night, and when the Simpleton would go into one of his trances, Saad would become exasperated. He no longer hesitated to chase him outside, even if it was snowing — especially if it was snowing, for Saad thought that the snow would calm down this madman. He said the cold calms crazy people down, he'd seen that when he was in the war.

"And so we'd be alone around our fire, the Nubian and I, and we'd wait. . . . Yes, at that point we'd begun to suspect that something was coming. Behind all that solicitude, all that consideration . . . behind all those hymns of frenzied admiration for that supreme president off in his capital, consumed by worry for his subjects stuck out in the middle of a desolate and endless stony waste. And one day the truth finally came knocking on our door and revealed itself. Straight to the point. It was as plain to see as you are now, right in front of my eyes.

"The hypocrite said to Saad, 'So, this card — you'll take it, then? It would make Monsieur the President so happy!' The Nubian, I needn't tell you, doesn't beat around the bush. 'If this president is as great as you say he is,' Saad replies, 'then why would he need a poor cripple like me?' And the hypocrite says, 'Monsieur the President needs all his children!' And the Nubian answers, 'I'm Nubian and black — so this president is Nubian and black, too!' And the hypocrite, still wreathed in smiles, still the wolf in sheep's clothing, his specialty, says: 'Monsieur the President doesn't have only one child. We are *all* his children, blacks and whites, young and old — and the Party card is our link with him!' And Saad replies, 'But he's in the capital, while me, I'm here, worlds and worlds away from him. How is the Party card going to link us together? It's impossible!' And the Delegate says, 'Nothing is impossible when it comes to Monsieur the President! He carefully saves copies of our Party cards in his marble palace by the sea, and these cards bring each one of us to his august attention. We are all his beloved children!' And the Nubian replies, 'For me — I'm telling you with my utmost respect — my life is here, in Lion Mountain. When in the winter the cold becomes icy wind, I touch myself and then I know I'm alive. When the sun is an oven in the summer, all it takes is a single breath of cool air: I wipe my hand across my brow, and there again, I know I'm alive!' And he adds, 'I need Horia, and the Simpleton, too, even if he is crazy now and then. Horia needs me, needs us — the three of us are just fine like this. Really, tell this president, and please tell the Party as well, not to worry too much about me. Thanks!'

"And that's how Saad came to grief. One day this spring, he went off to the livestock market to select some ewes from among an outstanding flock said to have been brought up from the Great South by an enterprising merchant. He did not come back, and there's been no news of him since. It's been more than two months now. . . ."

❖ 17 ❖

I ASK Horia why she didn't say anything to me in her letters.

"And worry you?" she replies. "Isn't it enough that harm has come to us? I should bring you into it as well?"

I knew that argument by heart. It's useless to discuss this point any further. I'd be better off thinking about what I can do now that I'm here.

Having learned from experience, I don't want to ask what her intentions are or risk letting her know about mine, which I'd decided on as soon as she'd finished describing the circumstances of Saad's new disappearance.

She has already guessed my intentions, however. I could see it in her eyes when she looked at me with affectionate approval, as if to say, "This time, I couldn't bear to interfere with your decision. Let's not talk about what you now see as inevitable."

I've barely had time to refresh myself when the imam is already here, arriving to welcome me home as he does each summer.

The vibrant, pale-purple light of late afternoon is the same; the fragrances of the imam and the perfumes of mint and jasmine on the patio are the same; the aroma of the rose water–flavored coffee is the same; nothing has changed in all this eternity. And yet. . . .

The imam will notice one difference from his last visit: this time Horia has hurried off to leave me alone with him.

It's because she's afraid — and rightly so — that he would reproach her angrily for her actions if she were to remain. Already crushed by her burden of pain and sadness, she preferred that the imam's disapproval of her silence regarding Saad's suffering both this summer and the last be voiced while she is well out of earshot.

I tell the imam everything I know. He listens attentively, idly fingering his prayer beads, without once interrupting me.

I try to set the facts before him, only the facts. I report what I've seen, what Saad has confided to me, what Horia has just told me, and I remain calm, trying to recount all this as clearly as possible.

The imam's solemn silence helps me to view this tragedy in a cold, dispassionate, clinical light. What other attitude can one take when dealing with gangrene? Isn't it vital to take immediate measures to combat the disease? When the imam finally speaks, I soon realize that he shares my opinion.

"Ah, that daughter of the Ouled El-Gharib! She

never changes. Always immured in silence, the silence of a descendant of noble ancestors. Tomorrow it could be the Flood or some such disaster, but it would never occur to her, not for an instant, to ask for help from her neighbor, even from me. It's intolerable, intolerable," he mutters.

I point out that Horia was perhaps confused by the imam's own counsels of prudence, which he gave when this business of the Party cards first came up.

"No!" he replies vehemently. "No! There's a difference between prudence and submission to tyranny. There is only one response to injustice: absolute refusal."

"Imam, the fact remains," I continue, "that your attitude was interpreted differently. People probably said to themselves, why resist if the imam is giving his blessing to the whole affair?"

"Me? My blessing?"

"That's how they saw it," I insist. "You really can't be too harsh with Horia now!"

"Is it giving consent to throw a dog a bone to chew on, to keep him busy so that he'll leave us and our doings alone? That's giving one's *blessing?*" protests the imam.

"From the looks of it, we're dealing with a mad dog."

"And how could I have guessed that, my son?" sighs the imam, obviously embarrassed, upset at the thought that he might have made an error in judgment.

❖

MANY years later, he would admit to me that he had never expected to hear such news when he arrived at our house. That was why he'd been struck immediately by a certain tension in the air, by the barely concealed sadness he'd seen in my face and in my welcome, by Horia's obvious nervousness and almost mechanical movements as she bustled about with but one thought in mind: to serve the coffee and quickly disappear.

He would tell me that he hadn't been overly concerned at not having seen Saad for the previous two months. In the past, when spring chores demanded his attention — and spring was the busiest time of the year for him — the Nubian had often been obliged to devote all his time to Horia's property, so that he was hardly ever seen in the village, disappearing on his own for weeks at a time. For his part, Imam Sadek had long ago given up trying to convince this servant of the daughter of the Ouled El-Gharib to fulfill his religious duties, to attend at least the collective prayer on Friday at the mosque, where the imam might have had occasion to see him.

For all these reasons, the imam had not become alarmed. To have acted otherwise would in his view have meant yielding too quickly to panic, when there were no other signs that anything was amiss and that horrible things lay behind the absence of a man who had, in reality, disappeared.

Horia, who should have spoken out, had not done so. There was no doubt that she was seriously at fault.

As for himself. . . . He would tell me — again, many

years afterward — that he had looked deeply into the mirror of utmost sincerity and there confronted his conscience. For having preached caution, for having understood the villagers' profound desire for peace and a life without problems — since life was hard enough as it was — for having, in a word, played his role as the guide of his community, a role ordained by God and the ancestors . . . was he to blame? This was the question the imam put to his conscience.

Hadn't he noticed that as soon as the villagers had accepted that accursed card, the disquiet that had reigned throughout the entire week of the diabolical propaganda campaign organized by that fiendish Delegate had suddenly subsided, giving way to the customary indifference the village had always shown toward everything that wasn't itself, everything that wasn't purely its own concern? Lion Mountain couldn't care less about political parties, presidents, motherlands, countries, capitals, and white horses popping out of the sea. Imam Sadek was perfectly aware that the village had always done fine without them. And since the dog was only asking for a bone, in return for forgetting all about the village and leaving it in peace, wasn't it reasonable and wise to simply toss him one? That's all he, the imam, had ever advised doing.

No, he had not made a mistake. He was convinced of this, in his heart of hearts.

THAT'S what he will tell me, that afternoon, after a long silence during which he seemed to be elsewhere, with his eyes closed, his head slightly bowed, his delicate fingers furtively telling his beads, almost without moving.

"I did my duty," he says firmly, in that tone of absolute decision which makes him precisely who he is: the imam of Lion Mountain. "Obviously," he hastens to add, "I consider that I did not fail only within the limits of what I knew at the time. Do you think I would have remained silent if your mother had told me what was going on?"

"And now?" I ask.

"Now? I'll do my duty," he replies mysteriously, before taking his leave to go call the faithful to prayer at sundown.

Pausing at the outside gate, he turns to me abruptly.

"You're coming to Friday prayers tomorrow?"

"Yes, Imam. You can count on me," I reply without even thinking, suddenly filled with a mighty surge of hope.

THE FATIGUE of my trip, the blazing heat that day, the sorrow I'd felt after hearing Horia's story, my immense confusion at being confronted by such unexpected and unbelievable events on the very afternoon of my arrival from America — all these things had conspired to stretch my nerves to the breaking point, and I'd sensed this especially toward the end of my conversation with the imam, when I began to fear that I might show him a lack of respect by asking questions or saying things that I would later regret.

The memory of Saad's wounds, his burns and the

humiliation he had endured, the memory of my own shame and my own nightmares in America, all that unspeakable pain, and now Horia's story on top of that, had pushed me to the brink of rebellion. I was determined to avenge Saad's blighted honor and recover my lost pride in belonging to this village, this land.

Yes — why hide it from myself? — I had felt the mounting aggressiveness behind my words, which had begun to border on insolence, and now I was overcome with emotion, with relief at hearing the imam tell me he would do his duty.

Tomorrow, Friday.

At the mosque.

So I would be spared at least one painful dilemma, and I was almost in tears. "Yes," I repeated to myself. "I'll be there. I wouldn't miss this for anything in the world."

❖ 18 ❖

THE NEXT day arrived. Friday. The news had
spread throughout Lion Mountain that the imam was
asking all the villagers to come to prayers . . . *and bring
along their Party cards.* Something important would
happen at the mosque. What? No one knew, exactly.
Rumor also had it that the imam wanted *everyone* to
come, so that there would be a big crowd. He was count-
ing on each and every one of them.

People were curious, but completely mystified.
Was the imam now getting directly involved in politics?
Was it possible? Unless he'd had one of his dreams. . . .
He has them every so often, you know. Had the ances-
tors ordered him to do this? A revelation, in other
words. Unusual? Perhaps. A revelation, nevertheless.
We'll see, they said.

But why *as many people as possible?* Why did the

imam want the greatest possible number of the faithful to come to the mosque? All the same, it was surprising, this insistence.

Hadn't they had enough rainfall that year? Hadn't the village been spared — narrowly, but spared — the plague of migratory locusts? The cloud of insects had finally passed by some twenty kilometers away. For the fourth consecutive year, the swarm had ravaged the crops on the other side of the blue mountains.

"Can you figure it out, Fadil?"

"What about you, Midoun? Do you think that. . . ."

No, really, there was no catastrophe looming on the horizon, no threat to the village.

Now the last time — that had been different. The imam had launched the same appeal, and the faithful had converged on the mosque in a body.

"It was the year of that terrible wind of yellow sand, you remember, Safouan? That great procession to invoke God's mercy, remember? It took a long time for us to line up, and then we started out slowly from the mosque, with our banners leading the way, fiercely whipped by that accursed wind. It was different that time, and, anyway, God heard our prayers. . . ."

THERE were endless discussions in the street stalls, in people's humble homes, in the neighborhood restaurants, and on the terraces of the village's three cafés.

A few leading citizens had an "in" with "Pock-Face," as Horia liked to call "Monsieur the Delegate." Fadil, for example, the rich merchant who dealt in barley and dried fruit. And Midoun, the well-known tanner of goat hides and sheepskins. And old Safouan, who owned the only olive oil mill in the village and surrounding area. And a few others. They had acquired this privilege by vying with one another in the lavishness of their gifts and banquets, and by toadying shamelessly.

Each of these worthies tried to outdo his rivals by offering his own explanation of the mystery. Nothing serious had occurred in the village for a long while, so this enigma was all the more perplexing, and people crowded eagerly around these sources of enlightenment.

Fadil's theory is that the imam, in his wisdom, has come around to the idea that these new times are proving favorable to tradition and to the heritage handed down by the ancestors. It's a good bet that in his sermon he will announce . . . *an alliance with the Party*, mark my words. Strengthened by this show of support, the Party will lead Lion Mountain toward a shining future hitherto undreamed of. Sly fellow that he is, Fadil concludes that there'll be something for everyone in this new development. . . .

According to Midoun, the Motherland is in danger. His information comes from *Monsieur the Delegate in person*. This danger threatens from the Great South, source of all their problems. The enemy will attack any day now, and proceed up Highway 15 to the capital. . . . *Monsieur the President himself*, yes, *himself*, has sent a secret emissary to the imam to pay his presidential respects to a noble descendant of the learned warriorlords, of course. After the ceremonial greeting, the emissary, in the name of *Monsieur the President,* urged the imam to mobilize the courageous sons of Lion Mountain to defend the Motherland. The imam *will first verify that everyone has his Party card,* added Midoun. *That's the least he can do to get things started.*

As for old Safouan, he maintains that according to ... *Monsieur the Brother of Monsieur the Delegate* — "a close friend, a man in the know about many things" — people in *high places* have recognized the important role the learned warrior-lords have played in history. Some highly qualified foreign specialists have recently arrived to announce some extraordinary news to *Monsieur the President.* Just imagine: they've found evidence of the epic adventure of the ancestors of Lion Mountain in books in German, Italian, French, and English. They've traced them all the way back to Andalusia. The books in question speak of magnificent palaces over there, of a mosque that still exists in Toledo and rises majestically at the edge of a large wadi always filled with water. *Monsieur the President* was very impressed. As the man of far-reaching vision that he is, he has decided (still according to *Monsieur the Brother of Monsieur the Delegate*) to curry favor with Imam Sadek, to whom he will entrust the post — or rather, the honor — of "Inspector General of the Party in Lion Mountain. . . ."

And old Safouan makes it very clear that *Monsieur the Brother of Monsieur the Delegate* was personally informed of these details by his sister-in-law, a very influential woman, as you can see.

❖

THE SIMPLETON was the one who reported all these rumors to us. I've summarized them here, and I've also organized them more coherently, because our informant was somewhat overexcited.

He imagined *Monsieur the President* making his triumphal entry into the village on his intrepid charger, wreathed in white clouds, his head high, his eyes searching the horizon for the minaret of the little mosque of Lion Mountain. The Simpleton was sorely disappointed that Saad wasn't there to join in the festivities.

Horia had wanted to send him back to the market to buy some flour he'd forgotten to get when doing the day's shopping, but he told her that all the stores were already closed. People were upset and confused, their nerves on edge, and had rushed home to wash up and change before hurrying off to the mosque, for no one wanted to arrive late.

What should she do? Horia had promised the imam honey crepes for supper that evening. Instead of changing her plans, she dashed out the door, exasperated by the erratic and impossible behavior of her foolish servant. It wasn't long before she returned empty-handed, forced to admit that the Simpleton had been right. The poor man then became agitated and fell into one of his trances, his eyes gleaming with a strange happiness.

"The village is completely deserted," Horia tells me, and now she, too, is filled with anxiety. "From time to time a swirl of dust and yellow sand suddenly forms here or there, whirling around and around as though driven by the Devil himself, a violent spiral rising

101 ❖

imploringly into the sky. Or else a stray dog wanders by, panting with thirst, dazed by hunger and the heat. May God protect us," she adds with a sigh. The imam would have his honey crepes some other day. "You ought to get ready," she tells me, "or you'll be late yourself."

❖19❖

FINALLY, I arrive at the mosque. The main prayer hall is already almost full, and the faithful are overflowing out into the courtyard. They continue to pour in, billowing, white-clad figures, cool and fresh from the Turkish bath. Yet they seem impatient, even a little worried.

As you cross the threshold of shining stones, worn and polished by time, you plunge immediately into a strange and unexpected atmosphere, heralded by the heavy odor of incense. It's more than the aura of contemplation you sense at the entrance to any house of prayer. True, there is that heady smell of incense, but there is also the unusual presence of candles glimmering in the corners of the hall. There are the clan's imposing battle standards, lying spread across the ancestral tombs, where their vast swaths of color still somehow gleam brightly, kept alive and shimmering by the centuries gone by. There is that sea of white at prayer. All this creates a heightened sense of expectation, of imminent crisis. Important events are about to take place. Earth and sky have joined forces. They have come together here, in the realm of invocation and defiance, and anyone who might think that the learned warrior-lords have abandoned their descendants would be grievously mistaken. The mosque seems to attest that there is a limit to provocation and injustice. This village has resisted the assaults of a thousand other hardships. And it will resist this time as well. Ancestors, awake!

The faithful are deep in prayer, their heads bowed. Few look up when I try to make my way to a favorite spot in the middle of the hall, where I used to sit leaning back against a column. I overhear Fadil murmur to his neighbor, "Look, there's Horia's son." Fadil is no doubt surprised to see me. I haven't set foot in the mosque in years, and my presence here surprises me just as much as it does him.

GRACEFUL and at ease in his white robes, the imam rises and slowly, solemnly, ascends the mihrab to deliver his sermon. At that moment, time, space, and all our hearts are gripped by eternity. One senses that for the faithful, from now on each word will be the Word, each gesture the Word made flesh; for them, everything has been poured into the crucible of the sacred. Yes, each and every word spoken by the imam will count. Sitting by my column, even I used to say to myself, "May God be with us, may He keep us free of all sin."

❖

THE FAITHFUL are now listening as a single soul, drinking in the words of the imam. There is complete communion between that peaceful white sea melded into one spirit and the deep voice, hesitant at first, but soon to be transformed into thunder.

I had lost my faith a long time before, so I pay little attention during the entire beginning of the imam's sermon, a commentary on a precept of religious practice. I glance carelessly around the hall, now and then contemplating some familiar object with nostalgia.

Suddenly, I note a battered old suitcase of a faded orange color sitting on the floor, hidden in the shadows behind the mihrab.

Is the imam going away somewhere right after the service? I'm surprised to see this incongruous object. But only for a minute. It slips quickly from my thoughts, for I am as if hypnotized by what I have been privileged to live in this unique moment.

The coolness of the ancient site doubtless helps relax the senses and dissipate one's concentration. The mosque, which is several centuries old, is protected by thick walls of stone hewn from the ocher mountain and whitewashed each summer. A few narrow, clumsy-looking windows are the only opening to the blazing heat outside. The interior of the mosque produces an exquisite sensation of well-being.

And so my attention continues to wander as the imam speaks to his flock, although a few words do sink in from time to time. It's the music of his warm voice that I listen to more than anything else, that captivating gentleness intent on guiding, on pointing out the proper path — it's that voice above all which holds me, pleases me, lulls me. My thoughts are elsewhere. . . .

ALL AT ONCE the calm sky is shattered by the rumble of storm clouds and the crackle of lightning bolts. I see a finger suddenly thrust accusingly at the peaceful white sea, pointing at a face which only the man thundering high up in his mihrab seems to see and recognize.

I turn my head slightly.

Pock-Face is here, too.

That infamous man, Horia had called him.

He is the one singled out by the imam's wrath.

❖ 20 ❖

"YOU WHO are true believers, you turn to me in time of need, when the road is not without pitfalls. You seek my advice on earthly matters. You feel yourselves caught in the tightening grip of this base and treacherous existence; you're afraid of suffocating, so you come to me that I may help you breathe. Then you return to your lives of toil, trying to forget your cares and sorrows. Yes, believers, you do all this, and it is only natural. As for me, my role is to act as a guide for my community, and this, too, is natural, for I am your imam. I would have you know, however, that I use no power, no magic, nor any kind of learning to show you the light. My conscience is my only source of wisdom. It is my well, and be assured that only in those depths do I seek. And what do I hope to find? My reflection, my face. The face of my soul. I question this image: 'Image of my soul, do you behold me with pride, or are you going to cast me off because I may be about to commit an error?' If my image returns my gaze with a steadfast eye, without trembling, without wavering, then I know I'm on the right path and that the advice I am planning to give you is sound. Then I may speak with a clear conscience.

"More than a year ago, remember, you were confused and came to me saying, 'Tell us, Imam, whether or not we should accept this card the new authorities are forcing upon us!' In prayerful meditation I contemplated the face of my soul and then gave you my answer.

"Today I confront the following dilemma. A true believer, one of your brothers, honest and innocent, loyal and courageous, is at this very moment being subjected to the cruelest of suffering. Look well about you in this house of God: your brother, Saad, the Nubian, is not here with us at prayer. Neither have you seen him, moreover, for many weeks. Do you know where he is? In the hands of a government that pretends to wish us well. Only pretends. In reality it seeks solely to dominate. And if it cannot achieve its ends by modest means, by gentle pressures, it doesn't hesitate to resort to harsh and bloody methods. It cuts backs to shreds, burns living flesh, degrades human beings — indeed, it stops at nothing. Let he who resists beware! Your brother Saad had the misfortune to say 'no.' At this same instant he is suffering the fate of those who dare to say 'no' to this power.

"And so, my faithful flock, here is my dilemma: I know two things at present and am torn between them. On the one hand, I know that everything that has any connection whatsoever with this government is from this time on stained with the blood of your innocent brother. The Party card you are now carrying is also stained with this blood, believe me.

"On the other hand, how can I forget that this village has experienced a relative tranquility? After a few weeks of disruption and anxiety, you took my advice and accepted this accursed card, and peace was restored.

"Now, what should I do? Remain silent? But how can I close my eyes to such evil? My well of reflections tells me 'no.' Yet if I ask you to throw away this vile scrap of cardboard, I risk exposing you to trouble. Have I the right to do this? Believers, such is my dilemma.

"So I turn to you: what should I do? Each one of you has your own well deep inside you, silent and clear. Seek out the face of your soul ... and give me your answer."

THE HALL is absolutely still. One cannot even hear the congregation breathing. People would remember this extraordinarily moving, unique moment for years and years. The imam was *beseeching* the faithful? That was unheard-of. He was visibly torn with anguish.

The villagers are even more amazed when the imam suddenly begins a dialogue with them, an event also unheard-of in the whole history of Lion Mountain. The ancient hall will resound with this unusual exchange as with the rumblings of a storm long trapped by stifling heat within the walls of a deep, narrow valley. The congregation's response, a single, powerful voice, explodes each time in a thundering chorus.

"I appeal to you, true believers. Are you prepared to help me?"

"Yes!" answers the chorus.

"After you have seen your spiritual face reflected in the depths of your inner well?"

"Yes!"

"In your soul and conscience?"

"Yes!"

"Then tell me: the cards you carry with you at this very moment, are they not stained with innocent blood?"

"Yes!" replies the chorus without the slightest hesitation.

"Is not complicity with evil a sin?"

"Yes!"

"Now, tell me: what do you need in life? Life itself?"

"Yes!"

"Air?"

"Yes!"

"Water? Sunshine? Light? The good earth of this village?"

"Yes!"

"And who gives them to you: God or this Party?"

"The Lord, the Almighty!"

"Do you need this Party?"

"No!"

"Then what must we do?"

"Tell us, Imam!" implores the chorus.

"Let me first address the representative of this Party, who has come to pray among you in the mosque of your ancestors. You should know, Sir, that before you there were Infidels here in Lion Mountain, but they understood that they had to respect the will of the learned warrior-lords, not interfere with the affairs of their descendants, and stay a good distance away from their village and mosque. When it has been proved to us that any successor to the Infidels possesses greater virtue than we do, more compassion for our neighbors, and a greater wisdom than ours, then we will bow to your intolerable efforts to meddle with our fate."

"God bless you, Imam!" resounds the chorus.

"God bless you, believers, and show you the way," continues the imam, trembling with conviction, choking back his sobs. "May He save you from sin!"

"God bless all true believers!" cries the chorus, sobbing in turn.

"God bless you, my brothers in faith," replies the imam. "May He protect the innocent man who now suffers the worst agonies inflicted by an arrogant government! May the Lord return our Saad to us alive — and let despotism beware!" shouts the imam menacingly to Pock-Face, on whom all eyes are fixed in a single accusing glare.

THE IMAM then calmly came down from the mihrab, picked up the old suitcase, opened it, and delicately set it down wide open on the tomb of the first El-Gharib ancestor.

"We will fill this suitcase with the sinful cards," he declared emphatically, in the familiar trenchant tone that meant his mind was quite made up.

But had he ever really hesitated in his decision that

day? Had he ever doubted his flock, feared, even for an instant, that they would not follow his lead? Why that suitcase, if he had had the slightest doubt? I still ask myself these questions today, without being sure that they matter in the end. Each of us is alone before our spiritual face, the imam used to say. . . .

IN ANY CASE, the anger of Lion Mountain's moral leader had struck home. The man whom Horia had gleefully nicknamed Pock-Face was dumbfounded by the temerity of the imam he'd believed quite tamed by flattery. He watched with mounting terror as one by one, the Fadils, Midouns, Safouans, and all the other important villagers, once so docile, now led the rest of the faithful to the suitcase, into which they tossed their cards disgustedly. Then Imam Sadek shut the suitcase and went to lay it solemnly in front of the Delegate before calling us to rise for prayers.

❖ 21 ❖

AND SO the new authorities had beaten a retreat,
leaving Lion Mountain in peace. For a long time, in fact.
Out of a desire to avoid trouble? Or perhaps — according to one rumor that enjoyed a brief vogue — because
the village's dossier had been misplaced in the capital
at some point during the many purges that were forever
disrupting the nation? No one will ever know.

AFTER that Friday afternoon at the mosque, the Delegate had disappeared. The headquarters of the Delegation itself — the former police station — had closed its
doors and fallen slowly into disrepair, unnoticed. Along
with the rest of the former French quarter, moreover.
Only the little hotel and a few poplars survived. In
short, Lion Mountain had reclaimed its destiny, and

things had returned to the path traced for them by the passing centuries.

Released from prison, Saad had taken up his life again at the point where it had been broken off. Out of a sense of decency, people were careful never to mention his nightmare. One forgets horror, Horia used to say. Why revive the pain with words?

Time had thus forcefully reaffirmed its eternal preeminence and function: to glide by. Just simply glide by. Flowing like the carefree little stream that runs past Horia's house, in the tender evenings and magical mornings of the steppe. Flowing like the seasons of the world, in the blood-red and golden air, in the rustling leaves of enchanted orchards. Flowing like life and death: flowing softly, imperceptibly, irrevocably.

And so those who were meant to grow old grew old, those who were meant to die passed away, and Lion Mountain endured, wise in the ways of confronting its ordinary hardships: plagues of locusts, sandstorms, and other calamities both large and small that the village knew so well.

FOR HORIA, the unhappy parenthesis was now closed, and on the day when it was Little Brother's turn to leave home, and he set out for Paris, she had felt a great sense of relief. It is written in human destiny, she often told us, to grow old and await death. Now that her two sons had left the village to become "doctors" and escape the injustices of the times — when people feared neither God nor man, she claimed — then what was left for her except to grow old calmly, to live in peace with life and the expectation of death?

BUT YOU know as well as I do, Little Brother, that Horia's peace and quiet will last only as long as you wish it to. You won't write, you won't come home for a visit — or only rarely — and when you do, each time you'll arrive with a new girlfriend on your arm.

Then there was May '68, further misfortunes, and years later came the time of bloodshed, when Horia was in the twilight of her life.

❖22❖

MAY '68, which you, with your romantic and es-
thetic ideas, tried to export to this shore of the Mediterranean, and that's how you came by your death
sentence. Then Palestine . . . the Khmer Rouge . . . Horia
was right: the ancestors protect you, there's no other
explanation. . . . I've lost track of your causes, your rev-
olutions — all lost, but that's another story.

OH, THAT SUMMER! Whenever I think of it, I feel a shiver
of dread and rage course through me! I was on vacation, on a small, isolated island off the coast of Florida,
in search of peace and quiet. No one could reach me,
and it would be too late by the time I learned about
the martyrdom Horia had suffered through the cruelty
of men.

She had begged them to let her see you before your

execution, but they had refused adamantly. Crazed with despair and howling out her love for you, she had knocked on every door. Have only a touch of compassion! A mother who holds her son in her arms for a few moments and bathes him in her tears before he's dragged off and put to death — that has never posed a threat to any power in the history of the world. It made no difference. They had remained deaf to her pleas, stonily indifferent to her pain. Worse, they'd forbidden her to come near the prison and had ordered the police summarily to chase her away if she showed her face.

BUT YOU had performed your most mischievous exploit, almost as if to justify Horia's faith in the promise given by the learned warrior-lords.

Playing on the naive piety of your jailers, two big country lads more thickheaded than evil-hearted, you'd used your inimitable skills and imagination to paint them a grim picture of the tortures awaiting those who do not perform their ritual prayers according to the prescribed norms. Said prayers must be offered up at the *exact* moment of the day or night assigned to each one, without the slightest delay, and must *never* be cut short or interrupted by anything connected with this world here below, not even the presence, in their cells, of prisoners in your charge. "When you stand before the Almighty, what use will you have for a good report card from a worldly power?" you asked your jailers, taking care, however, not to overdo it. . . . But your subtle hints finally took effect, and your guards were now following your advice to the letter. And so, after being a revolutionary leader in Paris in May, there you were, an imam on your native soil in July.

YOU FIGURED that your best opportunity for escape would be at dawn. At any other time during the night, your guards would sound the alarm if you were unlucky enough to awaken them by making too much noise. With their attention completely absorbed by their prayers and ecstatic devotions, on the other hand, they wouldn't let themselves be distracted by anything, not even the ultimate assault upon the government they served and which put bread in their mouths.

Dawn offered another advantage: the approaching daylight would welcome you, allowing you to melt into the early-morning crowd as soon as you reached the street.

Since they were sound sleepers, your guards didn't usually hear the muezzin's call, but that was before they'd fallen into the clutches of their new imam. Their old habit was to awaken at sunrise, and for the most part they spent only a few minutes at their prayers.

From now on they have to deal with hell — the Little Brother version. The dawn prayer — *and especially the dawn prayer,* you point out — must be performed at *dawn,* and if one wishes to curry some divine favor in these treacherous and uncertain times, one is strongly advised to prolong the prayer itself with subsidiary invocations and a recital of several verses of the Koran for at least . . . *one hour.* . . . Time enough for a quick-thinking prisoner who has perfectly prepared his move to break out and begin dreaming once more of some other revolutionary upheaval elsewhere.

EVEN Imam Sadek had approved.

Horia, whom you arrange to meet clandestinely at the border at night, in order to reassure her and say good-bye, comes with the imam and the Nubian. She holds you in her arms for a long time and kisses you, weeping, saying over and over, as though to comfort herself with this certainty, "They saved you. They've saved you again."

But she's disturbed when you relate how you escaped. By betraying the good faith of his two jailers and using religion for impious ends, hasn't her son committed a grave sin?

The imam sets her mind at rest. "Don't be afraid," he says. "God is on the side of the mother who is reunited with a son who has escaped an unjust death. He is, I would add, on the side of a mother reunited with her child *whatever the circumstances.*"

The imam uses his Friday-sermon voice: his tone is decisive.

"I had no choice," you tell Horia humbly. "I just didn't want anything to go wrong."

The imam agrees.

"You are right, my son. God permits many things when the adversary is a government that has lost even that minimum of humanity, compassion. He allows us a lot more latitude than we generally realize."

Then a faint smile spreads across his venerable

face, a smile of both happiness and amusement. The imam is probably thinking of the unlikely schemes you invented, with God's help, to fool your jailers. . . . He's imagining them carried away by their frenzied invocations while you clamber feverishly up the walls of freedom. . . . He can't help it; he bursts out laughing.

AFTER that night, Horia leaves your safety in the hands of our wonder-working ancestors. She will see you twice more, in all, each time at the border, and at night. She is at peace with herself and the fate she has accepted with serenity. Courageous, admirable woman. Then you disappeared for good. . . .

LITTLE BROTHER, do you know how our mother met her end? Do you know what Horia was driven to by her love for a mountain, for that pure line of horizon?

III
Blood

❖ 23 ❖

I UNDERSTAND why you didn't receive any of my letters. It was baffling, because I'd certainly sent them to you. Saad had put on the correct postage. You were as astonished as I was, that summer two years ago. You'd told me that not one had reached you, neither the ones in which I asked you for news of your little brother nor any of the others. I was prepared to put the blame on our Saad, if you remember. Could he have neglected to put on the right number of stamps? Thank God I didn't commit such an injustice. I'm glad that I believed the Nubian. Now it's all quite clear.

My information comes from Midoun's grandson. You haven't heard this yet, but his grandfather managed to get him a job as a mailman. They say the old miser shelled out the biggest bribe of his life, and no wonder, if you consider how fond he is of his only grandson, who, like all of you, is fascinated by foreign countries. Midoun was bound and determined to keep the boy with him during his declining years.

A good boy. He hasn't forgotten that when he was very young, my remedies cured him of a serious illness or two, and more than once saved his life. He's still grateful to me, very attentive, respectful, and affectionate.

He came to see me the other day. Late, at night. Secretly. After taking all sorts of precautions to make sure he wasn't being followed. First he made me swear on both my children's heads that I wouldn't tell a soul. Then he said to me: "Horia, you know that I love you as much as I love my own mother. I've always admired both your sons, too. As a child, my dream was to be like them. I'm heartbroken at the misfortune that has befallen you, and have often wondered how I could help you in some way. The moment has come: it's a perfect opportunity, and I'm not going to let it pass. You should know that the letters you write to your eldest son in America, and the ones he sends you, are all intercepted, by me, under instructions of the postmaster, who is himself acting on orders from the capital. The letters are then handed over to the Delegate. I assume the bastards are trying to trace the whereabouts of your younger son, now that there's so much talk about him in the newspapers. Those people are completely unscrupulous. I've heard it said that their killers are operating throughout the world, and that the President flies into a rage at the mere mention of your son's name. Be careful, Horia. . . ."

I listened to him in amazement.

Very straightforward, that young man. And what

courage! When I think of how his grandfather so often tried to ruin me! You were both so young then, and I was defenseless. God forgive him! And his grandson turned out to be so honorable! A generous soul. He truly feels for me, or why else would he take so many risks? He promised me he'd find a way to read your letters in secret for me.

He'll figure out some way. You're a doctor. I'm sure you know what I'm talking about.

I swore on both your heads that I wouldn't breathe a word of this to anyone. Except Saad. And Imam Sadek. I did tell him. I have absolute confidence in both of them.

What a world we live in! Why are they hounding us? An old woman who's only waiting for her time to come.

That's how it is. The Lord will judge us all, one day. Fortunately, there are some people ready to do good, like the tanner's grandson. Let's take advantage of this. If you have any news about your brother, send it to me.

Needless to say, the President and his people tell nothing but lies about my son. He's off somewhere studying to be a doctor, following in the footsteps of his older brother. He's more intelligent than they — which is why they don't like him. My son isn't hurting anybody. These people and their newspapers are lying. What I wouldn't give to hold him in my arms for a moment before my time comes. . . .

❖ 24 ❖

READ. Read, Little Brother, and may your terrible, your all-consuming anger, the rage that day after day is now resounding throughout the planet, devastate these accursed lands with the furious flames of a vengeance that will sweep the earth. Such is my ardent desire.

Your last appearance, you remember, was during that winter three years ago, when Horia was already so old, weakened by the relentless burdens of a hard life, diminished by the long succession of misfortunes. Yes, so frail from that time on. So fragile. Shrunken. Nonexistent. A shadow. The shadow of her former self, of the Horia El-Gharib of earlier times: vigorous, solid, energetic, the very image of a strong-willed woman.

The woman whom the men of Lion Mountain had become resigned to treating as an equal, one of them — this woman was gone. Cruel adversity had triumphed over her tenacity. When she spoke now, it was only to sigh. Profound, poignant, unbearable sighs. She spoke very little; she didn't like to complain. As old as she was, she still had her pride. She would often pray; prayer filled most of her waking hours. And she would gaze at the Mountain. . . .

❖ 25 ❖

YOUR LAST letter brought light to my life. May the Lord bless and keep you, and protect your wife and two little girls from harm.

The news you sent me of your brother brightened my heart, warmed the bones of your old mother, who patiently awaits her end.

I was right to think they were lying about him. He a terrorist? A killer? I was supposed to believe those despicable newspapers? Imam Sadek, who is writing this letter for me, is also reassured. He knows your little brother's piety, his goodness. The imam never attached the slightest importance to all those slanders. We thank you for these good tidings.

I hope that your little brother, as a worthy descendant of his ancestors, will continue to seek wisdom and knowledge wherever he may find them, so that one day, like you, he may finally become a doctor. Thus both of you will be your mother's joy in this life as well as in the next.

As for us, there is little to report. Nothing of interest. This winter is dragging on forever. Only the tourists (who are invading us, literally) seem to like it. The imam tells me they come for the sun. It's true, we have plenty of sun. As for Saad, he thinks they're attracted by something else. The village. The people. The colors. We seem strange to them. One always finds other people stranger than oneself. There they are: they never get tired of looking at us. They look at me, I look at them. They smile nicely at me. They're pleasant enough, I must admit.

All the same, the world is full of surprises! To come from so far away. Those cars. Those buses. That noise. That frantic activity. That exhaustion. To leave one's country and go wandering around in a wasteland, right in the middle of nowhere. And why? For the simple pleasure of looking at us — at us, at Lion Mountain. Can you, you who understands so many things, explain that to me?

They take photographs. Smile at you like children. They're charming, no question about it. Sweet. Little lambs, I'll grant you that.

For several years now, more and more of them have been arriving with each passing winter. Highway 15 at the foot of the Mountain is becoming more crowded. In this part of the village, which is deserted the rest of the time, your old mother suddenly finds herself with lots and lots of company on her land. The caravans of cars and buses stop in front of our house, forming a camp, as the camel caravans used to do in the time of the French, when Lion Mountain was still in the alfa grass business. You see their women — you know the kind — tall, blond, with hair the color of wheat, like your wife and little girls have. The men are in shorts, insensitive to the cold. Sometimes there are children, too. All of them gaily run down to our stream to refresh themselves, so full of life. So happy. Could they be from another planet? Then they fan out through the village, laden with their cameras, to . . . *look, take pictures*. I wonder what they find here that's so admirable. Everything is ocher. There's so much light! Nothing that isn't transparent, ephemeral, inexistent, worthless. Nothing. What is it, then? Explain it to me.

But they seem to like it, that's their business, and they're not hurting anybody. It's actually a relief to your mother to have them here. Incorrigibly enterprising even in his old age, Saad brings some of them to the house from time to time. They're delighted. Children, I repeat. They like to touch everything, are curious about everything. Fascinated by my kilims. Take pictures of everything. Above all, they're just as interested in your mother's ancient face, which is nothing but wrinkles, ravaged as it is and shrunken by age, as they are in all the rest.

I offer them mint tea. They're absolutely thrilled. Clever old Saad, who had something in mind all along, now makes his move. He asks them if they can discreetly take care of mailing from their own countries these letters I've been sending and that have been reaching you for the last few months. They graciously agree without asking too many questions. Very well mannered, these people. What a godsend!

We're expecting even more of them to come to Lion Mountain next year. Saad even saw — yes, *saw* — the name of our village printed on a map. With his own eyes. It seems a tourist showed it to him. The Nubian told us that he stood there gaping as this same tourist flipped through a little book with photographs, in color, of the learned warrior-lords' mosque. And the Mountain, too. Saad swore before the imam that he'd definitely recognized them. There's no reason not to believe him. This world is so strange.

If only these tourists could teach our authorities, and especially our madman out there in his marble palace by the sea, how to show more humanity to their fellow men! I'd pray to the Lord and our ancestors for the salvation of these foreigners' souls.

Let all the tourists in the world come here. I'd offer them my heart, my kilims, my land, my life if I could see, be it only for a moment, your little brother once more before I return to dust. If I could hold him in my arms. Just touch him, for one fleeting instant. . . .

❖ 26 ❖

IT'S BEEN a long time now since you've heard from us. There weren't any tourists, you see. Highway 15 was closed. Divine will has so decreed.

For more than a week the Lord drenched us with cloudbursts. At one point we thought we were back at the time of Noah. What torrential rain! It's a good thing the tourists were smart enough to stay home. All the wadis flooded. Whole flocks, goats, sheep, camels, swept away. Hundreds of trees uprooted. The deluge. The universe in a rage. Was God telling us something? What? Your mother will soon know, when she has crossed at last to the other side. I've been getting ready to go for most of life now. Perhaps then the Lord will consent to enlighten me.

As for Midoun, he's already gone. He caught a cold during this recent bad weather. He hung on for three days.

Finally gave up the ghost, the old fox. Almost a century of fighting and scheming on this earth! Pugnacious to the end, tight-fisted like nobody else. The imam and I are going to miss him.

He was my toughest enemy, but I admit that somewhere deep inside of me, I liked him. Lately, before the rains came and carried him off, he'd taken to visiting me in the afternoon. I enjoyed spreading a kilim out for him in front of the house, in the sun, and fixing him some mint tea. We'd sit there, miles away from everything. Two little old people at peace, reconciled. We'd spend long hours like that. Looking at the Mountain and the fine, superb light. From time to time, one or the other of us would say a word. Otherwise, we were just happy to still be here, simply to exist, and to admire that marvelous gift from the Lord and our ancestors — our beautiful Mountain. I wonder what our dear Midoun will be looking at from now on.

Not many people are left. They're thinning out, inexorably. All gone. Yesterday Safouan, Akermi, Fadil. Today, Midoun. The young people, too, but they're going somewhere else, and for a different reason, which I can understand. The trip we old people are taking is the last voyage. Once on board you find there's no turning back, not ever. Then we can see our struggles and sorrows for what they truly are: paltry things. We're all brothers and sisters when the final hour is at hand.

Your mother forgives everyone: Midoun, Safouan, the others. Yet I'd never say that they didn't fight me. As hard as they could, too! Even ferociously! I still wonder why to this day. But what's the use; the past is the past. By God's grace, a human being is able to enjoy happiness and wisdom, all because of that extraordinary ability with which the Lord has endowed him: the ability to forget. To forget. To forgive.

Still, I trust God will not hold it against me if I don't forgive the madman in the marble palace! To have deprived me for more than five years now of the sight of your little brother! Is that human? No, Lord, I'd rather go to hell than forgive that tyrant, who actually takes pleasure in seeing an aged mother like me suffer. Forget what they've done to me? Never. I'd rather go to hell!

Don't worry too much. Your mother's bones are still intact. I can still drag this old body around. In the evening now, at nightfall, when darkness envelops everything and sleep eludes me, I hear something like a bell ringing faintly. The Sly One playing me her dance of death. The Beauty of beauties. She passes furtively, all draped in black like the night. A playful, cavalier ceremony, the kind she's so good at. She doesn't dare come forward yet and pounce on me. First Safouan takes off. Then Akermi. Fadil. Now Midoun. Little signs she's making to me, at a distance, the pretty one.

In the meantime, the sun is robed in all its glory.

The weather is lovely this morning, clear and luminous as though the world had just been born to clarity and light. The torrential rain has washed the air clean. Carefree, the little stream is humming along and your old mother, her eyes fixed on the Mountain, is surprised to find herself feeling — why not admit it to you? — a kind of contentment. If I could just see your little brother again one day, even if it's only for a moment, before I, too, must leave.

❖27❖

I'VE JUST HAD a terrible dream. It has frightened me out of my wits. Your father: tall, imposing, resplendent in his mustache. Superb, radiating youth. Flashing eyes. He seems in a hurry. Each of his gestures, each word he speaks reflects his impatience.

A crowd behind him, a short distance away. They're waiting for him. Some partisans, clearly excited. He must be their leader. Midoun is there, too.

Your father comes toward me, drawn by a photograph. Of *you*. Published in a newspaper lent to me (in real life) by the new Delegate — I'll tell you that story some other time.

Your father points to the photo and suddenly says, as though to reproach me:

"Your son? Still *asthmatic* but covered with glory. He must join us quickly. We need him for the great battle."

"The *great battle?*" I repeat uneasily.

"The just will crush all the unjust beneath fire and blood, and the earth will quake," he replies.

Since I don't understand, he leans tenderly toward me, delicately takes my face between his large hands with their long fingers, those hands I haven't touched in more than forty years now, and in a voice choking with emotion, longing, love for his children and for me, from whom he was so cruelly separated, says to me: "Horia, forgive me for having left you alone for so long. You've suffered so much. Suffered so much," he repeats. "The time of blood has come." And I awoke shaken, completely distraught.

I woke up Saad. We spent the rest of the night in prayer.

Tell me quickly, tell me that nothing has happened to your little brother. Tell me that everything they say about him is pure slander. Tell me he's still alive. Your old mother is wasting away with sorrow and desperate love. I have the feeling that I'll never see my son again. . . .

❖ 28 ❖

STILL FAITHFUL, that young man. He regularly passes your messages on to me. I pray the Lord that nothing will happen to him. He's taking real risks. The imam is just as aware of this as I am. He also prays for our young mailman. God in his justice sees that the righteous are rewarded.

But while it may well be our fate to expose ourselves to danger, why should you come here to put yourself at risk as well? Stay where you are. Don't come home. We agree on that point: Saad, the imam (who is writing this letter), even the Simpleton, and I, naturally — we all give you the same advice. Give it up, I beg you. These people will stop at nothing. The news is not good.

Your mother's life is no longer of much value; I've had one foot in the grave for a long time now. Their crimes can't touch me anymore. I no longer need anything but the pure air of this village, my view of our beautiful Mountain, the sweet company of the stream, the dawn that welcomes my prayers each morning. These treasures are beyond their reach. They can never steal these from me. The Great Madman would have to usurp God's throne before he could do me any more harm.

My dearest possessions are a gift from the Lord. He alone commands the air, the horizon, the water, the dawn. No, don't worry my son. Your old mother is from this point forward an impregnable fortress. Only your return home could possibly rekindle the burning anxieties that would once again threaten to consume me.

Now you are both out on your own in life. Please, let me live out my last days in peace. Hasn't my heart bled enough, haven't I suffered enough? The waiting, the anguish, the fear, the sorrow — didn't they tear your mother's body and soul to pieces during those long days and nights spent before the prison in the capital? No, my son, this harsh torture which even the demonic Satan would be incapable of dreaming up for his enemies, this black time of contempt must never come again. Have pity! Pity!

If I go on at such length it's because — and this is what I couldn't spell out for you in my last letter — the new Delegate has warned me to be careful.

He's our third one since the shameful flight of Pock-Face, with his suitcase full of Party cards. This man seems good and upright. Very pious. He's at the end of his career. They say he took the post with us, out here in the middle of nowhere, for the purity of our air. On that score, you have to admit it's unlikely he'll be disappointed.

Quite portly. Heavy-set. A large, jovial face. A snowy head, both hair and beard. He inspires confidence immediately. His prayer beads always in hand, a compassionate word always on his lips. One feels that everything he says comes straight from the heart. When he encouraged me to accept this honest soul's invitation, Imam Sadek assured me that it was inconceivable that a man like that could be capable of treachery — the imam was sure of it.

I accepted. I went to the Delegation to meet him and his family in their home on the second floor, which serves as their official residence. I took along with me one of my old — and most beautiful — kilims as a gift.

They welcomed me as good people do, with exquisite courtesy. Consideration. Respect. Sincere kindness. Proof that in the world we live in, nothing is all white or all black. Pock-Face and the Great Madman do exist, but they are not everything. When drawing the boundary, one must consider only the humanity of each heart. There is no question that this particular Delegate belongs on the side of mercy — it was clear, one could sense it.

He spoke to me admiringly of you. I was surprised that he'd heard of you. He showed me a magazine in which people had written in praise of you, and there were photographs. I recognized you, in spite of my weak eyes. You, standing beside some famous people, it seems, in America.

I explained to him that you were a scholar, a doctor, but that true renown may exist only in the sight of the Lord. You were carrying out your mission here below, that's all — as it is the duty of each being on this earth to carry out his own particular task, humbly, without making a fuss.

He replied that I ought to be very proud of you. That the whole country ought to be proud of you. Then he said, "Alas, the fame of your American son" — so you're *American* now, are you? — "plus the disapproval voiced in high places of your younger son's regrettable activities, give pause. The capital does not necessarily feel either the same sympathy or the same enthusiasm for brilliant destinies as does a civil servant on the eve of retirement like myself. One might even venture to imagine that those in the palace are offended by your son's celebrity. My advice," he concluded, "is that he should stay in America. He should not plan on visiting you, at least in the near future. One never knows what might happen."

There it is. I beg of you. We all agree on this. Although I'm coming to the end of my road, yours has hardly begun, and the whole world lies before you. Why offer the Madman a golden opportunity to put a stumbling block in your path, as he has already tried to do — unsuccessfully — with your little brother?

You set out in search of wisdom and knowledge; out of sacred duty you have become an exile. Are we not all exiles upon this earth? Is not dust our natural abode?

From you I expect nothing else besides purity of heart. Kindness toward the weak, those of tender years, the aged woman, and the once proud man, humbled and brought low. Believe me, nothing brings us distinction in this life, be it here at home or abroad, except our humanity. Remember Monsieur Faure.

❖ 29 ❖

NO WORD can convey all words. One page, even a thousand pages, a thousand letters cannot contain what a flood of words can never express: love, longing, a swollen river still trapped in the deepest channels of the heart. We will go on writing to you, for we have no choice: pent-up emotions hurt so much. Everything would be different if fate had decreed otherwise, if you were here, before my eyes. Almost two years without seeing you! First your little brother, now you. Dear God, I'm only a poor mother!

Forgive me for venting my pain; the imam encouraged me to. It would be a sin, he assured me, to hide my sorrow from you.

It is for another reason entirely, however, that I hasten to send you this letter by means of a tourist couple who will be leaving tomorrow. It's to let you know about the strange rumors that have been circulating in the village for the past few weeks.

Saad tells me — and the imam confirms — that the growing reputation this accursed hole lost in the middle of nowhere has acquired among tourists is drawing the attention of the capital. That's all we needed!

Ever since a book — illustrated with *photographs!* — and a film — in *color*, they say! — came out abroad featuring this pathetic scrap of desert, the Great Madman has been having fits. It seems he would like to beautify us — yes, *beautify* us.

They say he wasn't exactly elated by the incongruous spectacle of those caravans of cars and buses, those women and children, that motley horde of frantic tourists tumbling in from the four corners of the earth to *camp out* — that was supposedly the way he put it — at the foot of the Mountain on your mother Horia's land, in its natural state: without any shelter, without so much as a café, a restaurant, a hotel, or anything to prettify the place and proclaim to the entire planet the unparalleled glory of the Madman in the Palace.

People say he has watched that damn film some Germans made dozens and dozens of times, and each time he hits the roof. And can you imagine — that nice, honest Delegate, who once invited me to his house, has had to pay the price: the poor man was quickly bundled off into retirement (some say into prison) for letting foreigners circulate such a "scandalous" image of our country. It seems the Great Madman is ashamed of us.

To cap it all, Pock-Face — after an absence of almost twelve years! — will soon be back. "Monsieur the

President," as that miserable lickspittle used to call him, is confident that the iron hand of the infamous wretch will soon straighten everything out. This is the *imminent* catastrophe everyone is talking about. Will the Lord ever have pity on us?

The imam — I feel no qualms at having him write this — seems resigned. *Times have changed,* he keeps telling me. *We've had our day in the sun. Most of the older villagers are gone, while the young people have scattered to the four winds. Let them hand over what's left of the village to the tourists!*

Fine. But they should leave us in peace for just a little while longer! Don't we have a right to the dawn, to the twilight in our last hours? Even stray dogs are allowed the freedom to die gazing at the horizon. Are we even less than dogs, then?

❖ 30 ❖

CAN YOU tell me what it is your father wants from me? After more than forty years he finds a way to reappear. He keeps coming back, night after night, saying the same thing over and over again: "The time of blood has come," worrying about me, his eyes brimming with tears. Can't he wait? So impatient, that man! He takes it into his head to wake up *now*, when my days in this world are numbered. What's come over him? Why has he, too, come back to hound me?

What have I done to you all to deserve this?

Your little brother, who vanished almost eight years ago and has forgotten that his mother has a heart!

You, who insist on wanting to come home, paying no attention to what I say or plead, condemning me to one sleepless night after the other.

The imam, who criticizes me constantly, calling

me "obstinate," "defiant," telling me that I'm being "difficult."

Have pity on Horia! Have pity, Lord!

Is it being *difficult* to announce in no uncertain terms that I refuse to give up my land? That I refuse to allow anyone to try talking some *reason* into me? That no one may touch what God and my ancestors gave me unless I agree to it? Isn't it clear? And plain, as plain and open as the stretch of land running from my house to the Mountain?

Nothing has ever obstructed that view. The truth is crystal clear, like the waters of the stream. Where is the flaw in that truth? Tell me!

I'm certainly not going to play at being a wise old lady at this late stage of my life. Do you expect me to start now embellishing the truth? To be worthy of my *great age* — as the imam says? Don't be silly!

The imam . . . I just don't understand him anymore. What does he want from me? That I should call *black* something that is *white* simply because I'm almost eighty years old, and when old ladies reach that exalted age, everyone expects them to be docile and uncomplaining? That Horia should suddenly announce: *white is black?* That I should proclaim, flying in the face of every truth: *life would be more beautiful if at dawn, at twilight, I could no longer see the Mountain in front of my home?* That I should say: *what belongs to me may be taken away from me without my consent?* And that I should submit to this simply because I'm so old, and because at my age, to take such an attitude is a sign of *wisdom?* Ridiculous!

I'm going to tell you exactly what the imam said

to me — don't worry, he's not the one writing this letter, it's Midoun's grandson.

Here are Imam Sadek's very words, just listen: "Horia, our time is past. You have worked, struggled, made the earth shake beneath your tread, caused men to tremble before the fire in your eyes. That was when time was on your side. Now the moment of parting is near. The earth will remain after your passing. Your sons have gone, never to return. So what is the use?"

"What is the use?" I replied furiously. "Imam, I don't recognize you anymore. Is this the imam who once thundered against injustice? The imam who drove out Pock-Face and avenged the victims of wrongdoing?"

"Our time is past," he muttered — that's all he could find to say.

After which he goes off to complain about me to Saad, telling him that for some time now, it seems, I've been *pigheaded*, obstinate, impossible.

Saad replies that it's my land, after all, and that it's my absolute right to let the authorities have it or keep it myself. The decision is mine.

The imam agrees. He admits that the law, ancestral documents, public opinion, the consensus of the village elders, all these are on my side. The problem lies elsewhere.

"Where is it?" asks Saad.

And the imam trots out his prize answer: "Our time is past. What must change must change — why fight it?"

Saad can't get over it either. He thinks their so-called *tourist area* is an intolerable scandal.

A gas station. A café-restaurant. A four-story hotel.

A crafts center. All that in front of Horia's house. Next to Highway 15, on the land between the road and the Mountain. On my land. Between my house and the Mountain. I would not see the Mountain anymore. Can you imagine what a blow that would be? Is that fair?

To deprive me of my beautiful view, after having deprived me of the sight of your little brother? Why don't they simply blind me? Murder me instead of murdering my view of the Mountain? The times will change, as the imam seems to hope — but before they do, let my sight be veiled, let night fall upon my eyes!

No, never! Never! And if your father must be right, so be it: let the time of blood come!

❖31❖

ONCE AGAIN it's Midoun's grandson who writes this for me. The imam is avoiding me. He never sets foot in my house anymore. He talks about me everywhere, telling anyone who will listen that I've lost my head. Horia has gone crazy.

When I go down into the village, people turn away from me. Horia, the plague, the raving lunatic. I'd lead the village straight to disaster.

The cowards! They sell, they sell, they pocket the money and sell some more. They'd even sell their souls, their wives — Horia, the madwoman, is keeping them from raking it in.

Pock-Face, yesterday in disgrace, is now famous. He has put on some weight, filled out those once hollow cheeks, acquired a Mercedes, and his respectability is at its zenith. Why? He's bringing those idiots a café-restaurant, a gas station, a four-story hotel, and a shop where they can sell off their kilims, their souls, and their wives' honor.

It's crazy Horia who's standing between Lion Mountain and *prosperity. Prosperity!* They parrot whatever the Great Madman spouts all day long on the radio.

When Saad suggests that they start out by restoring the ruins left by the French in the Spring, which would be perfectly suitable as a site for all those lovely things promised by the capital, they exclaim, "What? Clean up and renovate the tarnished past? No," they insist,"we have to start again from scratch."

"What do you mean, 'tarnished'?" objects Saad. "The French kept their distance from the Mountain, from the mosque, from the village, and they didn't touch a thing. They didn't spoil a single thing. What's been tarnished?"

In desperation, they fall back on what the imam has been zealously proclaiming in his sermons these last few weeks: "Times have changed, that's all there is to it."

They add that if *Monsieur the President,* acting on the advice of his experts, has chosen to endow Lion Mountain with a tourist area to be constructed on virgin soil at a geometric site — what does that mean? — it's because of his stupendous wisdom and foresight. He wants everything to glitter and shine: glass, concrete, and flashy shoddiness out in the desert. He, the greatest president on earth, means to have solid, tall, and breathtaking new stones soaring masterfully into the sky, singing to the sun and stars in praise of this splendid president and our entire glorious nation. . . .

"And where does Horia fit into all this? After all,

it's her land," my Nubian reminds them. "She would rather go on admiring her Mountain," he insists.

"Let her move her Mountain somewhere else," they laugh in reply. The idiotic laughter of the living dead. "Let her take it away with her and go somewhere else, off in the desert," they continue. "As for us, we absolutely must have the café-restaurant, the gas station, the crafts shop, the four-story hotel. It will be good for our wives and for prosperity. . . ."

That's the way things are at present.

❖ 32 ❖

YOU MUST COME — quickly, very quickly.

You're a doctor, you're an American, you haven't done anything, you're in newspapers, you're powerful — they wouldn't dare touch you.

Your mother is all alone, everyone is in league against her, you're all I have left. If God were listening to me, I'd say to Him, "Lord, you see this evil: why do You permit it? Make the earth quake, the skies resound with Your wrath, whirlwinds of sand rise up to Your throne, and the blue mountains crumble into dust! Do something, Lord! Show them that You will not tolerate tyranny!"

Can He hear me?

A swarm of strange people from the capital has descended like a cloud of locusts upon my land to measure, compare, evaluate: "surveyors," "engineers," "entrepreneurs," according to Saad. Everyone in the

village is welcoming them as saviors, celebrities —
you'd think they were royalty. Everyone's fighting to
claim their few moments of spare time, their little
smiles, their slightest gestures. Soon people will be offering them women!

The imam finally deigned to come see me . . . to
annoy and exasperate me once again. Who would have
thought it possible?

Imam Sadek, defender of the weak, of the child, the
orphan, the widow, who speaks with the voice of
God . . . has joined the others and gone over to their
side.

He pleads their cause. As for me, Horia, because I
refuse to let anyone touch my view of the Mountain, I'm
being an *obstacle to progress* (that's his expression). I'm
digging in, as he sees it, even though the world must
move forward, with or without my consent. He says I'm
forgetting that the living have the right to go on living.
I'm not taking into consideration the interests of . . .
future generations (his words again). I'm a stubborn old
woman whom he no longer recognizes.

I listened to him, but I was too upset to say anything.

These people all think that I'm already dead. They
haven't understood a thing. No, they never will.

So come and show them that *you* understand
Horia. I gave you life, and I've never asked you for anything in return. Today your mother stands alone against
everyone. You're all she has left, since your little
brother has disappeared.

You're a doctor, you have influence — come defend
your mother before it's too late.

❖ 33 ❖

HER CRY reached me many weeks later.

The well-meaning messenger who had agreed to mail the old woman's letter had probably forgotten it in the bottom of a suitcase, a backpack, or in the folds of a wallet. . . .

One of those innocent mistakes that can happen in life, but which are as if marked by an unavoidable curse of fate.

By the time I received the letter, the tragedy had already occurred.

❖34❖

THURSDAY, the day before the ceremony.

A crisp November day, luminous, metallic, cool but bathed in sunshine. There's magic in the air.

The festive atmosphere is almost palpable. Lion Mountain is getting ready. Happiness, excitement. Tomorrow is the "ground-breaking ceremony." The regional governor is expected to attend. Perhaps even . . . *Monsieur the President*, although it's not certain, a question of security, but still . . . perhaps. . . .

THE DELEGATE is having them build a triumphal arch, just in case. A modest construction, made from local materials. It's a bit clumsy, and not too sturdy, but as long as there's no big sandstorm it should hold up. The paint slathered on in heavy ocher brush strokes has dried, blending in with the rest of the landscape.

The President will arrive via Highway 15. He will drive by the ruins of the Spring, the former French quarter. His procession will pass the point where the road turns off and then continues on into the old village, where almost immediately it will come upon the triumphal arch erected in his honor.

The official portrait hasn't arrived yet, but the Delegate is expecting it at any moment. The capital promised it to him, so he's hoping to receive it sometime this evening. Whatever happens, the portrait will be — yes, *will be* — hung in time, assuming of course that "Monsieur the President" graciously honors Lion Mountain with his visit on this unprecedented occasion.

ALL THINGS considered, the village is fairly tidy. There was no need to whitewash the few outside walls that were not originally ocher — that chore had recently been taken care of during the summer. Sand has been cleaned off everyone's front doors. Some of them were badly faded from the blistering rays of the sun over the previous months, and have been repainted dark blue.

The stray dogs and alley cats have been chased off, sometimes killed, and the corpses dumped far away, behind the Mountain, to avoid the smell.

The many tourists are mingling casually with the population, as well as with the soldiers and a large contingent of plainclothes detectives dispatched by the capital at the urgent request of the Delegate, who wants to avoid trouble at all costs. That's the last thing we need, he keeps saying to himself, if "Monsieur the President" does decide to come to the ground-breaking ceremony.

People are selling, smiling, looking, taking pictures. Joy and excitement are everywhere. A few women have ventured outside — with the permission of their husbands, fathers, or brothers — which adds to the holiday atmosphere.

In short, the future looks bright, radiant with happiness. One day, perhaps, the young people who have left the village will have the wisdom to return, so that Lion Mountain will no longer belong only to the dead and the wandering tourists, dazed by the sun. Or so everyone hopes. This is truly "Monsieur the Delegate's" fondest dream, a vision he is proud to have passed on to "Monsieur the President," who has made it his own.

WORKERS are racing feverishly to finish building the grandstand that has been erected on Horia's property, right in front of her house. They're in a good mood, despite the pressure; everyone seems pleased. They'll probably be working late into the evening — all night if they have to, and why not? The future of the village is at stake.

A *tourist area*, here. . . . Who would ever have imagined it?

Certainly not the crazy lady. But then she's crazy, that's just it. Everyone thinks so. A question of age, really. Senile. . . .

Ever since the men set to work on the grandstand, by order of the Delegate, she's been watching them, like a stupid animal, in front of her house. She eats there, prays there, sleeps there — she's not budging an inch. Lost, bewildered. *Touched in the head:* it's hard not to admit it. Sad, but that's the way it is.

People say they tried anything they could think of to please her. Every important person in the village did his best. The imam. The leading citizens. Even "Monsieur the Delegate." It seems he suggested every possible solution, offering her a fortune if she'd agree to sell her land to the State. They say he even tried to tempt her with a presidential amnesty for her youngest son, if he's still alive. Nothing doing; she sits there, silent, her eyes staring at the Mountain. Like a statue, already dead. Finally they all gave up. Talk about stubborn! They'd never seen anything like it. Too bad for her!

FROM TIME to time, Saad passes by the grandstand. His hair is completely white; his posture slightly stooped, but vigorous. He has retained his strength and determination despite his handicap, even though old age has further slowed his already halting steps. Leaning clumsily on his crutches, he passes by with a quizzical air, now and then shaking his head unconsciously. Each time, he strikes the asphalt of Highway 15 so hard with the metal tips of his crutches that the laborers and the smattering of soldiers with machine guns who are guarding the work site inevitably turn and look at him. The sun glints off the guns of three aged tanks of Soviet manufacture, as old as the hills; one is aimed at the Spring, another at the minaret of the little mosque, and the middle tank points its gun in the direction of Horia's house, which is set imposingly in its universe of ocher against a background of pale green and, farther back, pale blue, then ocher again, with other unknown tints of light and dust sparkling in a thousand endless mirages, far, far away. . . .

SOMETIMES Saad turns back and hastens over to Horia. Standing motionless before the old woman, he observes her for a long time without saying a word. She, too, remains immured in silence, gazing fixedly at the diaphanous horizon, at the Mountain looming behind the partially completed grandstand. Each time, unable to bear the silent sorrow that torments the aged companion of his life, Saad suddenly strikes the ground with the tip of his right crutch, always with the same force, and then, as though possessed by a demon, returns to Highway 15 and to his mysterious, nervous trips in front of the workers and soldiers. . . .

THE OLD Corporal has come to a decision. To settle a score, to settle all scores. To take revenge for an injustice, for all the injustices at once.

He hasn't forgotten. Pock-Face. The cigarette burns, the rats, the humiliation. The shuttle of pain and infamy between Lion Mountain and the capital. The arbitrary tyranny of men.

He hasn't forgotten. . . .

Tears spring to the Nubian's eyes. So many injustices! Horia's heartrending pleas in front of the prison. The frail old woman's farewells to her son in the icy wind of the steppe, groping her way over the stones in

159 ❖

the dark of night. The worry, the longing that fills the heart with ashes.

And now, this. No, it's too much.

Saad's decision is final. He'll tell Horia about it tonight. Tomorrow, after the collective prayer in the mosque, those wicked men will have their "groundbreaking ceremony." That's fine. Horia and he will have *theirs:* to each his own and we'll see who wins in the end. . . .

❖ 35 ❖

AT NIGHTFALL, Saad returned for the last time from his strange peregrinations on Highway 15. He stopped in front of Horia.

"Daughter of the Ouled El-Gharib," he announced, "the dawn of the partridges is calling to us. Hold your head high. Together we shall gaze into the distance."

"What partridges? Have you gone crazy, too?" Horia answered, startled from her sad meditation on life and the cruelty of men by the loud voice of her servant.

Dropping his left crutch, Saad bent down to her with some difficulty and affectionately held out his free hand, helping her to her feet.

Then they both went inside, followed by the Simpleton, while Saad repeated in a low voice, as one might recite an old refrain, "The dawn of the russet-plumed partridges is calling us, the dawn of the russet-plumed partridges is calling us. . . ."

Horia still doesn't seem to understand the enigmatic remarks of her old friend. And why should she? Instead, she's rather irritated by the Nubian's apparent lightheartedness. Such whimsical behavior, such incongruous fantasies in a situation that demands silence, in the absence of sober speech and resolute action.

No, really, Saad's going too far. Horia finds that he's behaving strangely, to say the least. She looks at him and sighs.

"Once a child always a child. Even at your age."

SHE PROBABLY hoped that Saad would give way before her obviously immense weariness and fall silent, go to his room — without dinner, if necessary — and perhaps recover his reason in the healing surrender of sleep.

She so longs to be alone. She feels the weight of the entire universe crushing her. In the depths of her soul, with every fiber of her dilapidated body, she longs for only one thing: peace. Silence. She can well do without the Nubian's foolish ramblings, these incoherent stories of partridges and salutations from the dawn. . . .

ONCE THE two patio doors are firmly closed — the large exterior door of walnut, and the smaller, lighter interior door — Saad feels safe, safe enough to forget about the tanks and soldiers outside.

He asks the Simpleton to light a nice charcoal fire;

these early November nights on the steppe are quite cold.

Around the glowing, crumbling coals, around the flames like blood-red tongues of heat and light that play caressingly for hours across the anguished faces of Horia and the two faithful companions of her life, Saad now speaks plainly and with a terrible precision, his frightening words strangely mingled with more tender evocations, beautiful memories that remind Horia of a time long ago, a time of happiness and respect. Monsieur Faure and his gratitude to the Corporal who had left his right leg at Monte Cassino as a sacrifice for France. . . . The chief of police's unwavering kindness and consideration toward the daughter of the learned warrior-lords. . . . The surprise visits of the Frenchman, tightly buttoned up in his spotless uniform, at the wheel of his jeep. . . . Monsieur Faure's unexpected assistance in Horia's efforts to sell her bounteous crops of tomatoes, pimientos, and other fruits and vegetables in the most distant villages, beyond the blue mountains. . . .

"And do you remember, Horia," continues Saad as though inspired, "how you wanted to express your gratitude to Monsieur Faure, and how I suggested some live partridges, since he always dreamed of caressing their silken russet plumage whenever these handsome birds flew past in the scarlet twilight? . . ."

"Yes," answers Horia softly, as though her thoughts were far away, with her face so close to the voluptuous, spiraling flames. "I remember. . . ."

"And how from his mad hunt in the desert that morning, at the source of the spring that generously nourishes our land, the Simpleton brought back three beautiful, very beautiful partridges, trembling and magnificent, and how we offered all three to Monsieur Faure, like maidens of paradise, and how he loved them so? He was astonished, moved, delighted, and this unexpected present strengthened our friendship, sealing it for all eternity. . . ."

"Yes," replies Horia.

YES, YES, YES. She remembers all this enchanted past so well, and with her heart warmed by these memories of a happy time she had thought lost forever, now suddenly reborn out of the icy steppe and darkness, with her face flushed and reinvigorated by the glowing embers, with her aching soul slowly casting off her sorrow and weariness, the old woman will listen with distinct pleasure to her Nubian. The Simpleton will shed tender tears of longing and nostalgia. . . .

"THE RIGHTEOUS dawn also gave us a machine gun that day, do you know that, Horia?"

"A what?"

"A big gun. A machine that massacres, that kills."

"Kills *whom?*"

"A hundred men at a time. . . ."

"Lord! Preserve us from Evil!"

"At Monte Cassino, the war, the horror. . . ."

"Monsieur Faure's war?"

"A thousand soldiers cut to pieces, lying on the blood-spattered snow. Like worthless flies."

"Like *flies?*"

"I was king."

"*King?* You? A black?"

"A thousand cartridges. I could hear the crackle of gunfire."

"Lord!"

"And now, it's too much! Too much!"

"Where is this gun?"

"A machine gun. Well smeared with engine grease. In a crate. Protected. Safe beneath the big mulberry tree on the property. More than a thousand bullets. . . ."

"Smeared with *grease?*"

"The machine gun."

"Lord! And you're saying: *to kill? To kill,* right?"

"Everybody. Tomorrow. Aim at the reviewing stand, the Mountain, beyond. . . . Massacre at Monte Cassino for Monsieur Faure."

"Lord."

"Tomorrow. Pock-Face, the Great Madman, the imam if necessary. . . . It's just too much!"

"With the gun?"

"A big machine gun, I tell you. A monstrous machine that kills."

"A *big* gun?"

"Yes."

"To hunt men, not gazelles or partridges?"

"Yes, Horia. Yes."

"Where is it?"

"Hidden on the property, in a crate, under the big mulberry tree, I tell you."

"And you never let me know about it?"

"Forgive me, Horia. . . ."

"When they were hounding me, breaking my heart. . . ."

"The Lord. . . ."

"My son. My land. The Mountain. And you still feared Him, Nubian?"

"I hadn't given up hope. . . ."

"Nor I. Nor I. The heavens would one day take pity on Horia, you thought?"

"Not anymore. Too much is too much. . . ."

"Yes, Nubian, you are absolutely right."

"Tomorrow — the machine gun on the roof for their festivities and their ceremony."

"Lord! We implore thy mercy."

"Tomorrow. . . ."

"We must not offend God, Nubian. Let's not lose our heads. We cannot go astray tonight of all nights. May God in his mercy forgive us our moments of weakness and show us the way!"

"All of them, I'm telling you. . . ."

"All of them. And may the Most Merciful take pity on us and all humankind!"

"For justice. . . ."

"My son . . . my two sons. . . ."

"Yes, daughter of the Ouled El-Gharib, and for everything else. . . ."

"SO MUCH tyranny! Why does the Lord permit it? What have I done to Him?" cries Horia as she bursts into tears, choking with sorrow, trembling and moaning. . . . In all his long life, the Simpleton has never seen such abject despair.

❖

AND THAT evening, around the slowly dying embers, in the deep embrace of the cold night, all three of them let their sorrowful tears flow freely. A few moments later, they all withdrew in despair to their rooms, exhausted and bewildered, not knowing what the next day would bring: the Simpleton still remembers this clearly.

He also remembers that on that evening, contrary to the habit of an entire lifetime, Horia said none of her prayers. The Simpleton, the sole survivor of the tragedy, remembers this particular extraordinary fact with the utmost clarity, despite all the painful events that followed.

❖ 36 ❖

WHAT FOLLOWED that long, cold night spent around a charcoal fire in the heart of the vast steppe, when defeat, doubt, and despair were all arrayed against Horia, was this.

Saad and the Simpleton are abruptly awakened only one or two hours after retiring.

Horia's cries, curses, incantations, and commands surge and explode, shattering the fragile calm of the night and the dreams that stubbornly envelop her two servants in their soft cocoon. She seems possessed, unrecognizable, an untameable lioness.

"Nubian," she shouts, "Arise, the Deceased awaits me. Midoun awaits me, the ancestors await me. On your feet, Nubian!"

The Deceased? Si Taher, her husband. Father. He has just appeared to her once more. He is the one who has transformed her into this bundle of fiery energy that streaks across the suddenly frightened night. He is the one who has turned her into this Fury who makes everyone and everything around her tremble. Saad and the Simpleton are struck with astonishment and terror.

"The Deceased has spoken clearly," she continues feverishly, in great agitation. "Blood must flow and bathe the Mountain in its splendor. Quick, the big gun! There's not a minute to lose!"

Still in a state of extreme agitation, yet strangely sure of her vision and her words, which are unquestioned realities for her even though the rage that fuels them threatens, in these tragic moments, to swell, to explode into madness, she continues to harangue her two companions.

"Si Taher knows what must be done. He said to me, 'Set up the big gun on the roof of the house as the Nubian wished — we are all at war.' He said to me, 'The learned warrior-lords have awakened from their sleep of centuries past to come deliver you and avenge the Mountain.' And they were standing behind him, inscrutable, sitting majestically upon their impatient white Arabian stallions, ready to charge, with the banners of their clan snapping in the breeze. 'Defend what must be maintained intact — do not yield! Defend the ocher mountain!' He said to me, 'Though all else stir and change, the Mountain remains. She deserves our blood, and the time of blood is at hand. . . .' Get up, Nubian, and you, too, simple one!" she cries.

❖ 37 ❖

SAAD HAS no need of such urging. He had already made up his mind the day before, as I have said. Only his abrupt awakening prevents him for a few brief moments from realizing how much fate — or some other mysterious incomprehensible force, tending nevertheless toward harmony, equilibrium, and perhaps justice — has conspired to further his plan through the voice of the late Si Taher.

He says to Horia: "I'm ready," and once he has dressed, settled himself on his quivering crutches, and gulped down his coffee, he, too, will be bursting with energy.

The immense pain, the immense sadness that have consumed the daughter of the Ouled El-Gharib during these past weeks have lasted far too long, and Saad cannot bear her torment any longer. Thus he is now overwhelmed with happiness, exultant, ecstatic.

Saad is convinced — no doubt by his sixth sense, his sense of the fantastic — that the old woman has *lost her mind*. Driven crazy by so many injustices, so many misfortunes. Horia's madness makes him in turn literally wild with joy.

He has been waiting for this blessed moment for a long time, for twenty years, dreaming of going crazy one day and finally deciding to have it out with Pock-Face. Now, with those others, their tyranny. . . . He doesn't need Horia to urge him on.

❖38❖

AND NOW, at this late hour of the night, the three conspirators are more than ever united. Abandoned by the world, they turn their backs on it. Betrayed by reason, common sense, and the elementary demands of simple compassion, they reject them in turn. Scorned by men, they resolve to pay them back for every injustice. What else are bullets and machine guns for?

To settle a score, all scores, Saad has been repeating to himself for several days. No more compromises. Madness has set him free.

The three tortured souls of the night are now three rebels of the dawn.

❖ 39 ❖

THE MADNESS of that night opened a breach in the innocent dawn, which gave way before the inexorable events that followed.

From that moment on, what else could be expected of the day just breaking over Lion Mountain and its dream of festive ceremonies, except horror?

Such will be the fate of that morning on the sixth of last November, Little Brother.

AFTER having helped Saad fetch the machine gun from its hiding place under the big mulberry tree, lift it up onto the roof of the house, and carefully camouflage its position, all under cover of darkness, the Simpleton is suddenly struck with fear.

Strangely enough, in this black hour the sanest of

the three conspirators is this poor, simple soul, whose instinct for survival stands him in good stead.

The despair and madness of the other two rebels have less power over his naturally unbalanced mind.

When Horia and Saad, still obviously in the grip of their frenzy, announce to him at first light that Friday their intention to fight for justice by shooting anything that moves on the horizon, even if the soldiers across the way shoot back, the Simpleton feels as though a knife has been thrust into his belly.

The threatened animal in him springs to life, and at the same time — who knows how? — awakens other faculties that have slumbered quietly since his early childhood. A miracle, the imam will tell me.

The Simpleton does not want to die. He does not want Horia, whom he loves and respects, to die. He does not want Saad, who has always been his friend, to die. He must do something. Paradoxically, he begins . . . to *think*.

REFLECTING on the state into which his two tormented companions have fallen, the Simpleton decides that only the imam can prevent the tragedy.

So he finds a way, through some harmless pretext, to escape discreetly from the demoniacal watchfulness that reigns on the roof.

Thanks to the same ladder up which he hauled the machine gun on his mighty shoulders, he slips unnoticed back down to the ground, secretly leaves the house, hugs the rear walls to keep from being seen from above, and sets off at top speed, his long, powerful legs racing as they never have before.

 ❖40❖

WHEN HE listens to the Simpleton's story, the imam is at first incredulous. He doesn't believe a word of what his visitor is explaining to him with desperate but striking logic.

Quick, you must hurry — Saad and Horia have gone mad!

But there is the force of the images depicted, there is above all the amazing coherence of the words spoken in these troubling moments by the aging Simpleton.

A SENSE of urgency finally seizes the imam.

When I see him again a few weeks after the tragedy, he will tell me that he saw the hand of divine intervention in that strange and tardy rebirth of the Simpleton's reason. A sign. Doubtless a message from the ancestors, who meant to warn him, their holy heir, of an approaching catastrophe.

The imam hesitates no longer, and sets out with the messenger.

❖41❖

ON THE WAY, the imam decides to stop briefly at the mosque. A prayer of invocation to the ancestors would be a precious aid in this moment of peril.

He asks the Simpleton to go on ahead to Horia's house — he will follow him.

DRIVEN by the same animal instinct that had earlier led him to seek out the imam, the Simpleton leaves.

But he does not go home: he moves off in the direction of the desert and disappears. It will be more than a month before anyone sees him again.

❖ 42 ❖

THE IMAM is among the first to appear on Highway 15, which is deserted at that early morning hour. Even the tourists are still asleep.

He comes from the south and walks with some difficulty, leaning on his cane.

When his silhouette appears in the distance, he is still a long way off from the grandstand, and also a long way off from the tanks and the soldiers camping on Horia's property, who are slowly, peacefully beginning their day.

THE SUN has only just risen, touching the village with its first glints of gold.

The distant minaret of the little mosque is a thrilling sight as it gleams in the sunshine: delicate, beautiful, and alone.

❖   178

❖43❖

THERE IS no doubt that the first burst of gunfire from the roof was aimed at the imam. It missed him. It was quickly followed by a second burst, which misses him again.

The Corporal, obviously, has lost his touch. Monte Cassino is far in the past.

IMAM SADEK remembers having then heard a series of deafening explosions that shook the earth and the blue mountains, and he saw a gigantic cloud of smoke, flames, and ocher dust billow up from Horia's house into the placid sky.

ACCORDING to the inquiry, it would appear that a panic-stricken soldier had run to his tank, ducked down inside, and begun shooting like a madman at the house in front of him on the other side of the road. The house of Horia El-Gharib.